Harold Vallings

The Transgression of Terence Clancy

Volume 3

Harold Vallings

The Transgression of Terence Clancy
Volume 3

ISBN/EAN: 9783337390716

Printed in Europe, USA, Canada, Australia, Japan

Cover: Foto ©Andreas Hilbeck / pixelio.de

More available books at **www.hansebooks.com**

The Transgression of Terence Clancy.

BY

Harold Vallings,

Author of " The Quality of Mercy," etc.

"Good thoughts (though God accept them) yet towards men are little better than good dreams, except they be put in act."—BACON.

In Three Volumes.
Vol. III.

London:

·Richard Bentley & Son,

Publishers in Ordinary to Her Majesty the Queen.

1893.

THE TRANSGRESSION OF TERENCE CLANCY.

CHAPTER I.

THE trout in the Hollacomb canal had for many years been considered the most exclusive and aristocratic caste of the fish world in this neighbourhood. Cut off from the vulgar struggles and competition of the main stream, they had for generations enjoyed that combination of repose and good living which makes for high-bred serenity. As a man worried by small cares and heart-shaking bills waxes lean and bitter, and becomes a person to be shunned of his fellow-man, so a trout in a moorland stream, ever hungry, ever compelled to snap up every scrap of food that passes for fear it should go to fatten his neighbour, becomes a reckless, pushing, vagabond sort of fish, devoid of self-respect, hateful to his fellow-trout.   In this way it comes to pass that even a duffer may always pick up a troutlet or two in rapid broken water.   These youngsters, indeed, so far from having the nice discrimination of well-fed fish, will swallow down, without the least regard for prudence or decency, the scrubbiest bottle-brush of a hackle ever twisted up by a country tackle-maker.

Now, in the quiet-curving canal, especially in the upper reaches where it stole through the vicarage garden and the lush meadows below it, there were always to be had good feeding, bright water, and high-class society. The trout—few and fat, with beautiful waist-coats of white and gold—could live on sound hygienic principles; with leisure for proper digestion and friendly discussion. They were a class set apart and strictly preserved by the angling association, for the canal made an excellent nursery for the more vehement Chilling. No upstart from the river was ever admitted into this desirable residential preserve; and even such a traveller of note as a salmon-peal—should he chance to find his way under the canal hatches—was treated with a distant politeness that was apt to send him back, crestfallen and ashamed, and cynically craving for the free-and-easy society of the main stream. There had once been some talk of making the canal free water, of abolishing this house of lords at a swoop ; but Mr. Doidge, who owned the water-meadows, put his foot down at once, and wrote a scorching article in his newspaper—and so the scandalous suggestion came to naught.

Under the little foot bridge that connected the vicarage tennis-lawn with the other part of the garden there lived the reigning sovereign of these waters—a noble trout of full three pounds weight, who could take down two or three of the Chilling sprats at a meal, almost without wag of tail.

This lordly fish happened to be talking with a friend one afternoon, and from their conversation it might be gathered that blossom-time had come round again, bringing enlivenment to man, beast, and fish.

" Look here," quoth his troutship in fish-language, "they're actually beginning their insane tennis antics again—heaps of 'em on the lawn, d'ye see ?—and more coming. Faugh ! 'tis enough to spoil a man's appetite."

"They won't spoil yours, however !" thought the friend. " But, my dear sir," she answered aloud, " we shall see all the dresses and bonnets, which will surely be a boon ? "

" And lose the iron-blue dun ; just coming on thick, and the juiciest thing of the season ! "

he muttered bitterly. " But, as a female, you of course harp on the millinery ? "

" And you on the feeding ! " she retorted, with a pert quiver of her pectoral fins. " If you can't appreciate pretty frocks, why not go and spend the summer under the Holla-comb woods, Mr. Appetite ? "

This sally, however, was destined to pass unrebuked, for the sheeny little iron-blues came suddenly down upon the water, whirl-ing, flickering, dipping ; and the big gour-mand was at once lost in a gastric ecstasy that no insult could disturb.

While he lay under the bridge, sucking in the duns with an absorbing relish, half the youth and fashion of Chillington and its neighbourhood passed over the big trout's head ; for none could resist the first tennis-party of the season.

Mrs. French-Chichester was there, with a new *protégé*, lately promoted to her train, *vice* Terence Clancy deceased—at least,

married and done for.   This time the lessee
of her favour was a British subaltern, home
on sick leave—a man ungifted with Terence's
modesty, and so unable to resist the de-
bilitating effect of the great lady's petting ; so
that she had well-nigh rendered him unfit
for human society, and in another week or
two his attack of arrogance might, figuratively
speaking, be expected to end fatally.   But,
happily, she was going to drop him in a few
days ; when the fever might take a favourable
turn.

With them was Miss Tredethlyn, looking,
to be perfectly candid, not a whit less insolent
than the subaltern himself; for the atmosphere of a Chillington gathering was apt to
inflame her natural weaknesses.   She always
breathed the air of the town with difficulty,
and some of the commoner sort of people,
often to be found on the vicarage lawn,
affected her nervous system painfully.

Honest Mrs. Nelson looked wistfully at

Mrs. French-Chichester and Miss Tredethlyn when they arrived, as though to entreat them to be gentle with her humbler guests. But no gleam of pity was awakened ; the kind little woman abased herself for nothing. However, long practice had doubtless taught her the impossibility of pleasing more than about five per cent. of her guests ; and were she to leave the choosing of them to a select committee of her friends, why, hospitality would be a simple process. In such a case, her six children might chance to have the garden to themselves, with ices, cakes, and dainties enough to make every one of them ill for a week. As it was, she asked everybody she knew—and suffered martyrdom. And the hard part of it was that she was too poor to entertain at all. Public opinion compelled her to do so, then criticized her roundly for doing what she couldn't afford.

When Captain Rush came across those two ladies, with Mr. Pardington their subal-

tern in tow, his smile was grim and bitter.
He drew his father's arm within his own as
if to defy Miss Tredethlyn, and gave her a
bow to match his smile.

The subaltern, catching sight of Rush,
exclaimed to his companions—

" Why, that must be Rush, of the 20th
Dragoon Guards, one of the best polo-players
in the service. Had no idea he belonged to
these outlandish parts ; must go and have a
chat with him, by Jove ! Why, he rode one
of my ponies in a crack polo match once,
and I was doosid proud, let me tell you ! "

Presently, on the lawn where tennis was
beginning, Mr. Pardington had an opportunity of carrying out this threat. Rush was
standing alone by some rhododendrons when
the other lounged languidly across to him.

Mrs. French-Chichester, being now thoroughly tired of the youth, hoped to see him
snubbed ; and, reading Rush's face aright,
expected it. She glanced at Kate, and they

understood each other without a word, at
once making a detour round the rhododendrons, and so passing behind the two men.

The subaltern was commenting scorchingly
upon the play, the people, the rustic toilettes,
the vicar's old coat and baggy trousers, and
such things. Rush hardly looked at him at
first, but when he had quite done, said in a
calm reflective way, as though remarking
upon the points of a horse, "What a d—d
little snob you are, Pardington!"

Mrs. French-Chichester had to go further
behind the bushes to enjoy it. Soon afterwards Pardington joined the ladies, blushing
beautifully.

"Well, have you had your chat with the
distinguished captain?" asked the malicious
widow. "Did he put you up to any 'tips,'
as you call them?"

He only muttered something inaudible.

"Do you see that limp-looking old gentleman talking to the vicar?" she continued;

" that's Captain Rush's father, now Squire of Bickington—once a Bond Street tailor."

"Aha!" cried Pardington, cheering up swiftly, "I always thought Rush was a nobody. Somehow I never could be intimate with that man!"

" I suppose this is another Captain Rush?" Kate asked, in a steel-tipped voice. "Not the one who rode your pony?"

"Oh, er—yes—he's the same man."

"Your views seem to have changed rather rapidly?"

"Ha ha!" laughed Mrs. French-Chichester, charmed to see her *protégé* roasted. "When you grow to be a man, my dear boy, you won't be so ready either with your blame or praise."

" And if you wish to practise feminine spite, you should mix it with feminine wit," added Kate. "The one sounds so poor without the other."

" Come, cheer up—you boys do take a

snubbing so badly! Didn't he ask after your mamma?" inquired the elder lady kindly. "Dear me! men are so selfish; they forget these little things."

"Don't let us keep you, Mr. Pardington; you might like another chat with Captain Rush?" Kate's eyes sparkled. It was clear that she had not nearly done with him yet. In fact, the punishment went on for some time, till at length Pardington extricated himself and retired, feeling like a whipped puppy.

"That's right," cried the widow cheerfully, "we're rid of him at last; I'm sick to death of that boy! Now, Kate, let us go and have a good look at the interesting natives—they're worth it."

But Kate was out of tune with herself, her companion, and things in general. "How well he summed up that Pardington boy!" she was reflecting. "Even so might he sum me up, propriety permitting. But he won't come near me; he has done with me altogether, and it serves me right. I did want to talk to him about Simon, and we always agree upon that topic. I could agree with him upon almost any topic now—but, heigho! we shall never get beyond the weather again as long as we live, and—and what a flat, dull, stupid affair this party is—how I wish I had never come!"

She looked round almost wistfully for the soldier and saw him talking with Lord Bridistow, whose youngest brother was about to join Captain Rush's regiment.

Lord Bridistow was asking Rush, whose high reputation in the service he was well acquainted with, to advise and befriend the younger brother. The mild old Squire of Bickington was listening placidly the while, looking pleased and satisfied, yet not much puffed up by his lordship's almost eager civility to his son; for the highest honour shown to Julius could be no more than an incident in the general fitness of things.

He had no desire to talk himself, liking better to bask in his son's conversation ; yet was gratified to see Kate looking on from the other side of the tennis-court. And she perceived his complaisance, blushing inwardly. " He thinks his son will score a point in my estimation from being talked to by a lord," she muttered, "and doubtless he's right, quite right. How low an estimate of me, and how true ! How easily even a simple old man can read me ! Yet I'm not quite so bad as he thinks. Perhaps I'm like one of those American butterflies my father was reading about the other night, which, being good for food, mimic others that have a nauseous taste or smell ; but they do it for protection, while I have no such excuse. Ah, how gladly would I throw off my protective colouring !"

Her reflections were here cut short by the talkative widow.

" Kate, my dear, there's a woman here

whom you positively mustn't miss. She has disappeared for the moment; but I pine for her return, and will soon point her out. Don't ask me to describe her; just wait and enjoy her to the full when she appears."

A brisk four-game of tennis happened to be going on in front of them just now, and an ardent pair were running and striking between Kate and Captain Rush; yet she managed to watch him, and to note that he never threw a single glance her way. He smiled at one or two of Lord Bridistow's boyish jokes, and when he smiled Rush's somewhat sullen face brightened in a way which was apt to startle new acquaintances.

As she took in the pleasant scene, with its crowd of happy young people bathed in May sunshine, and backed by golden laburnum and a creaming wealth of crimson and pink May, poor Kate waxed sentimental.

> "Beamy the world, yet a blank all the same,
> Framework which waits for a picture to frame."

That was the colour of her thought, though she had not Browning's power of expressing it. The picture had not been wanting, had she not smudged its beginning like a naughty child; the May might have been in heart, instead of before her eyes, had she not checked its first growth. How proud—yes, *proud*, as she now confessed— would she have been to find herself pointed out by all these people as the affianced bride of a tailor's son. Ah, the laburnums would have gleamed then !

For a moment, for one moment, she caught his eye, and perceived how immediately the sullenness came back to his face. What a pity the weather was so fair ! she hated this spread of monotonous brightness everywhere. There was no character in anything ; the world wore a smile fatuous as that of a silly child.

These darksome reflections, however, were cut short by her companion's voice, which seemed thinner and more irritating than usual.

" Ah, *now* look, my dear; here's a farcical-comedy-in-petticoats, to be sure!"

A very large woman was sailing down between the courts, a woman whose coming stopped conversation to permit of hard staring; immense in point of height and breadth, still more in point of thickness, and dressed with bewildering splendour. Rather a handsome woman, too, though nature's efforts had been heavily handicapped with paint and powder.

" She was rubicund when I last saw her, but now her cheeks have what artists call a ' scumble ' of white—hence the delicate purple bloom," commented Mrs. French-Chichester, staring through her glasses with the pleased air of one who introduces a veritable phenomenon. " I believe Mrs. Ludlow, the Lymport milliner, contemplated suicide after finishing that bonnet; at least, I found the poor woman in a low hysterical state which alarmed me. She entreated me with tears not to let this headgear of Mrs. Saunderson's drive away my custom, but I reassured her and recommended a dose of sal volatile."

"Who *is* this Mrs. Saunderson?"

"The daughter of a famous house—a gin distillery at Lymport. I'm told a sister of hers married into serge the other day, and another into haberdashery; but she herself has been clever enough to secure a gentleman—Captain Saunderson, of the Royal Red Clayshire. He has had to sell out, of course. What married quarters in the kingdom could have held his wife? However, he's short-sighted almost to blindness, so he *may* not take to drink."

Conscious of the admiring gaze of a whole lawn full of people, Mrs. Saunderson now came floating down between the courts in full view of Kate and Mrs. French-Chichester. Upon reaching a point just opposite her critics; she halted and turned to a little man who must have been following in her wake, though hitherto hidden by her masses of drapery.

" Now, John dear," she said, " we must find my niece, Kate, and I'll introduce you to her. She'm here somewheres, I know, and what a fule I shall look if we don't find her ! "

Mrs. French-Chichester, gurgling with suppressed laughter, whispered with a neat imitation of the stranger's accent—

" Happen you'm the niece, my dear ? "

Mrs. Saunderson's voice struck the listeners with amazement. They had naturally looked for sonorous tones to match so ample a personality, but the voice was low and sweet, and had a ring of human kindness that accorded well with her infantile smile, suggesting the presence of a simple natural soul somewhere within that vast tract of millinery. The voice was that of a good-natured child, the intonation that of a kindly woman, the accent that of the back streets of Lymport.

Though the play was far from brilliant, people began to stroll up in twos and threes to watch the game on this particular court. Young Tom Nelson, the vicar's son, whose skill drew few lookers-on as a rule, began to wonder what had come to every one, to try and brace himself up to the level of this large audience; and the other three players did their best to back his gallant endeavours, until, flushed with so much flattering attention, they all four surpassed themselves.

Presently Mrs. Saunderson, after questioning one or two of those about her, resumed her triumphal progress. She marched down the court, worked her way round the end, past Lord Bridistow and Captain Rush, and turning to the left once more, bore down with full swing and sweep of all her drapery towards Miss Tredethlyn _and her companion.   The little captain again followed in his wife's wake, looking somewhat limp and spiritless.

Mrs. French-Chichester, eyeing him furtively, whispered—

" He *will* take to drink, if trotted about like this.   Has the woman no mercy ? "

A moment later Mrs. Saunderson stopped before the pair, exclaiming, with her smile narrowed a hair's-breadth by a touch of nervousness, " Kate, my dear niece, I've just come round to make your acquaintance ! "

What had happened ?   Had the sky fallen, or the earth opened, or the sides of the universe cracked ?   Was she falling headlong through infinite space, or had some one stunned her by an accidental blow ? Kate felt as though her consciousness were split open like a pod, and the shattered fragments flying round her.   " Niece— niece—*this woman's niece ?* "

The friendly smile was crumpled in a

moment, the good-natured face was purpling under its bloom, the large woman was panting audibly.

"I—you—you don't seem to understand. I'm your Aunt Mary, I am. Han't Mr. Tredethlyn, my brother-in-law, told you? Didn't he get my note this mornin'?"

Still Kate said nothing, but stood in a stupor of amazement. The would-be, or real, aunt paled again, and tears came to her eyes.

"I—I never thought," she whimpered, "as my own niece would treat me so, and me married to a gentleman! John dear, will you kindly explain to the lady who I be, and then we'll go, and never see her face again?"

But John Saunderson was too angry or too wretched to make explanations; and the vicar had to step forward from the crowd, for gather round they would, mere propriety shrivelled for the nonce by intense curiosity.

Before Mr. Nelson could open his mouth, however, the poor woman turned to him sobbing—

"'Tis gospel truth, it is; but I've no wish to claim relationship if my own sister's child don't want me. Ah, if poor Minnie had lived she'd never have brought up a daughter to set her lip at me that way!"

There was a time when Kate's first thought would have been to hurt and crush this woman who was covering her with ignominy, but severe mortification had brought with it some discipline. Julius Rush's resolute neglect had loosened her arrogance at the roots, and taught her the pleasing art of self-criticism. She could still carry an arrogant front, as we have seen, but beneath it a crumbling of old dogmas had been going on, and something like a creeping paralysis of her old self-confidence. Rush was in sight now, standing apart with Lord Bridistow instead of pressing in as others were doing, but she felt that he was listening eagerly, and wondering how she would come through the ordeal.

In truth, it was a miserable moment for Kate. Hardly any conceivable eddy of circumstance could have hurt her pride more than this public claim of aunthood by one whose outward woman was so crudely vulgar.

Yet she hardly doubted but that Mrs. Saunderson was speaking truth. A dozen corroborations of the painful fact were flitting through Kate's mind. Mr. Tredethlyn had always been reticent concerning his wife, insomuch that she had feared to press home any questions about her mother's birth and connections, fearing to hear of something derogatory, the while she proudly persuaded herself that there was nothing to fear. Yes; this degrading claim was but too probably a sound one.

The iron entered Kate's soul, but the gaze of many crities stirred her courage. No one could have felt worse; yet hardly any one, endowed with her special prejudices, could have behaved better. The pallor resulting from astonishment and horror gave way to a bright blush, and with a fine effort of will she spoke quite steadily.

" I was not aware that I had an aunt living other than my father's two sisters in London, but I do not for a moment doubt your word, Mrs. Saunderson. Your letter may have arrived by the midday post, but I have not been at home since the morning. I think you will pardon my great surprise under the circumstances, and—and, shall we shake hands ? "

Now was the sharpest pang of all, for the kindly woman fell upon her with a gush of tears; embraced her effusively; poured upon her a flood of talk, with its local accent strengthened and swollen by excitement;

and, in short, could in no wise make enough of her.

Captain Saunderson, who felt much for Kate—and would have felt more had his own misery been less acute—now came to the rescue. Never before had Kate quite realized the blessedness of what seems under ordinary circumstances but a mere outward grace—good breeding. Captain Saunderson, though quivering with discomfort, at once engaged her in easeful small-talk, and they were soon strolling away as though nothing had happened, the large aunt beaming beside them. There were tears of gratitude in Kate's proud eyes when she turned them upon the little captain.

The humble ex-tailor, Squire Rush, had listened to it all; horrified at his own ill breeding, but too poignantly interested to tear himself away. He looked wistfully at Kate every time he passed her afterwards, and many times muttered to his son—

"She's a grand creature, Julius; she came out, I say, nobly.   I don't often swear, but, *by George*, she's a grand young lady!"

Julius said nothing, but looked a year or two younger and five years less sardonic. He would have given much to be allowed to speak to Kate now, but this was not to be: she had to punish some one for what she was suffering, and at present he was the only available scapegoat.   If he drew near to her she looked more bitterly haughty and unapproachable even than in old days; and while Mrs. Saunderson prattled on, like a pleased child permitted for the first time to handle some rare and delicate toy, she comforted herself by plaiting together a few sentences by way of whip-lash for her father. For, though she was behaving so well in public, she meant to let flesh and blood have their say in her father's study presently.

There were some tolerably caustic things said about Kate as she walked to and fro with her new relatives; and the criticisms reached her nervous system, though not her ears. Tennis began again, and every face she met looked decently incurious now; but she knew that every eye was on her, that tongues of flame were licking her name. Briefly, Kate was under fire, and displaying not a little valour; with no prospect, as far as she knew, of medal, or reward, or even honourable mention. But she thought it due to her pride to remain on the field and take her punishment without flinching. Nor was the pain of her humiliation lessened by the instinctive perception that it gave such general satisfaction as that of no one else would have done; for was there a soul present whom she had not rebuffed or insulted at one time or another? Her friend Mrs. French-Chichester was unkind enough to commiserate poor dear Kate openly by glance and shrug; and went so far as to take back young Pardington into favour on

purpose to talk the thing over. Assuredly
the popular widow was not to be surpassed
in the useful art of extracting pleasure from
a friend's misfortunes.

Mrs. Saunderson's artless babble never
ceased, and Kate was speedily in a position
to comprehend her father's mysterious
silence.

Mr. Tredethlyn had, to summarize a long
story, married the daughter of a wealthy gin-
distiller of Lymport, thus making possible
his retirement from arduous parish work to
the pleasant haven of Moor Gates. His
bride had been anxious to cast off the fetters
of trade and become a lady outright, and he
had been quite willing to further so laudable
an ambition. Thus an understanding was
arrived at by which she paid stealthy visits
to her people now and then, but was left
unmolested by them in full enjoyment of her
new status. For their part they kept to the
bargain faithfully, and Mr. Tredethlyn had

seen little or nothing of them since his wife's death.

But honest Mary Saunderson, having so gallantly captured an officer and a gentleman —thus becoming as good a lady even as her sister had been—thought it high time to lay claim to the two handsome nieces whose fame had long since reached her ; and an invitation to a Chillington garden-party seemed to offer a delightful opportunity of achieving this end. Accordingly she had written yesterday, frankly stating her views, and thus giving the Tredethlyn party the chance of avoiding the meeting if they chose.

It will be seen that her innocent scheme had been all fair and above-board. With a beating heart, but a perfectly clear conscience, she had come over by train from Lymport prepared to embrace her nieces with effusion if they appeared, to try and forget their existence should they hold aloof from the

party.   Could they once make up their minds
to meet her face to face, she felt that, grandly
dressed as she was, arch and fascinating as
she could be, supported as she would be by
so unimpeachable a husband, she must needs
take even the proud Miss Kate by storm—
and this was just what she had done.

The Saundersons were among the last
people to leave the vicarage, and Kate stuck
to them to the bitter end.   They were to
return by a particular train, and so were
unable to accept an invitation she gave them
to accompany her home ; but some day the
new aunt, whose kind heart was drawing
Kate even in her humiliation, hoped and
trusted that she would be free to come and
pay Moor Gates a real visit.   This must be
deferred for a time, however, for the bride
and bridegroom were returning to town to-
morrow, and in a few days were starting for
the Pyrenees.   Dear John, as his attentive
wife explained, was so far from strong that

his doctor wished him to spend at least a year or two in a cheerful sunny climate.

"Dear John" winced uneasily while his bride was descanting upon his feeble health. The man was as strong as a horse, and knew that Kate was aware of it. Yet it was not mere shame that was driving him abroad, the truth being that he was in a peculiar position. He had sold himself for money and was being rewarded beyond his deserts, and far beyond his expectations. It was embarrassing, but true, that his wife insisted upon bringing him affection over and above the longed-for cash; which made him a mean fellow in his own eyes. For he was just sufficiently superior to the average man to kick against a bargain by which he took all and gave nothing; and his present intention was to take this affectionate bride abroad, especially to such places as lay outside the track of his fellow-countrymen; to get used to her; to make much of her—if possible, to get fond of her.   A good deal of this Kate gathered from his manner as she drove the . new relations to the station, and what she learned of the couple this one afternoon gave her much food for reflection afterwards.

When that bewildering thing, Aunt Mary's parting embrace, was quite completed, and they had stepped into the train, Kate gathered up her reins and drove off in an oddly mixed frame of mind ; but above the tangle of feeling produced by the almost tragical episode of the vicarage lawn, there stood up stiff and straight the desire for vengeance upon her father.   It comforted her soreness to think of the coming scene in that offending parent's study.   The black-browns were driven up the hill at a pace which astonished them.

Robbed, as she felt, of legitimate grievance against her aunt, the craving to punish her father increased with every yard she traversed. It was his weak, hypocritical silence that had brought upon her such humiliation as would make her quiver for many a long day : it would be a solace—some slight solace—to make him suffer with her. When she had spoken her mind, the balm of self-respect might, perhaps, be restored to her.

The black-browns smoked along the road, whirled round the short drive from lodge gate to front door, and Kate sprung out. The boy who took the ponies shivered when he caught Miss Tredethlyn's eye.

In a trice she was in the study. It was empty.

Her fierce peal of the bell was answered immediately ; her hopes dashed to the ground the moment afterwards.

" Master got a letter by the midday post while you was lunchin' at 'Ollacomb, miss, and soon afterwards ordered his things to be packed. He says you're not to be anxious ; but he feels a bit poorly and has gone off to the Royal Hotel at Lymport to get a breath of sea air for a day or two ; and will you please to send after him his—— "

" That will do—you may go."

Left alone, poor Kate could bear up no longer. She sank into her father's deep smoking-chair and poured forth her pent-up vexation in a flood of tears.

CHAPTER II.

"HARDLY ever, dear lad, do I venture to set up my opinion against yours. Come, now, am I a bitterly dogmatic father?"

Julius Rush smiled, though he happened at this moment to be in a mood more favourable to frowning. The father and son were traversing the long conservatory which bounded two sides of the drawing-room at Bickington; the former was pressing a point with all the mild warmth and gentle earnestness which he possessed.

"I think, I do think," the squire insisted, holding his son's arm tightly, and carefully adjusting his stride to suit the longer pair of legs—even as he always tried to adjust his thinking to fit the larger mind—" that Miss Kate would be pleased to see us. She must know that you care for her, though you have avoided her so proudly—not that I blame you, my dear son. No, no. I admire your pride and wonder at it. How different was I at your age! But, then, I was only a tradesman, for whom high spirit would have spelled 'ruin.' You're a gentleman; with every right to let your heart speak. Well, as I was a-saying, she knows you care for her; and she knows I'm not a bullying, hulking sort of fellow to go and crow over her in misfortune. I think she would take a visit from us as a mark of delicate respect; I do think she would understand my motive in coming, would see as I'm anxious in my humble way to show that my respect for her is only increased by what she has gone through. It might even draw her towards me a little; and that way lies your only chance, dear lad, for you'll never begin courting her in earnest until she's kinder to me—will you, now ? "

The taciturn captain smiled again at the old man's simple cunning, but the smile was not acquiescent.

" I agree with you," he said moodily, " as to the increased respect ; but it is so few days since that scene at the vicarage. Her pride will still be rankling, and she'll make a scape-goat of you, and insult you, and—and I shall hate her more than I do already ! "

" My dear lad, my dear lad," murmured the father with a kind of despair, "is it possible that you really hate her ? Why, she has never hurt me intentionally; it horrifies me to think that I should be the cause of your estrangement."

" Not another word, father. It is your persistent kindness that makes me hate her so."

The squire grew depressed and silent. He was too simple to comprehend his son, having no conception what pranks the " pangs of disprized love " play with a man. He felt altogether humbled and rebuked, and quite unable to reach up from his own mean level to the lofty mental plane in which his son moved.

"Well, dear lad," he concluded, with the patient sigh of a meek man who casts aside a cherished scheme, "you shall have your way; we'll keep away from Miss Tredethlyn. And you'll pardon your old dad for being so pressing?—and, pardon me again, dear lad, but if you pull the blooms from that azalea I shall have a dreadful time of it with McTavish!"

"Father," cried Julius, with a kind of wrench of his whole body, " I wish to God you were not so humble!"

"I'm sorry to displease you, Julius. I'll try and do better."

Then the soldier looked so black that the old man trembled.

" Those cursed servants," Julius muttered, with a slow flush creeping up his dark face, " have bullied every bit of life out of you."

The poor old squire was walking on tiptoe now, hardly daring to breathe. He felt the muscles of his son's arm tighten and throb.

Julius walked slowly on, with his face working. He had not been home for some months, and had now returned to find his old father a mere butt for the insolence of his dependents. The servants, pampered, spoiled, unchecked by any hint of the captain's return, had become little short of cruel tyrants to their master. Children, the butler, had a way of crushing him without a word, of letting him know by mere lift of eyebrow that he was but a tailor; and the others, perhaps unhinged by idleness, and the dulness of a country establishment in which little or no entertainment was done, followed Mr. Children's lead with tolerable success.

Things changed somewhat from the moment that the order for preparing the captain's room went forth, but respectfulness is not to be re-acquired at a few hours' notice. Julius, noting his father's increased timidity with the men-servants, and judiciously leading him into admissions as to what had been going on during the last month or two, quickly learned enough to make him rage inwardly. He yearned for vengeance ; but could catch no one actually tripping. He was as a steel-toothed trap set open in their path ; and they knew it. He had seen enough, however, to justify the dismissal of four or five of them, though his father shivered at so terrible a suggestion.

"What makes me so mad," he said presently between his set teeth, "is that you go through it all for *me*."

This was true enough, for the squire would long ago have given up this big establishment but for his desire to have a home worthy of his son and his son's friends.

"Well, Julius," he admitted reluctantly, "sometimes I do rather wish myself in a snug little villa, with two or three maids and a man. They—they *have* punished me somewhat of late. I almost think I could see my way to letting you remonstrate with Children and McTavish—not harshly, you know, but—— "

" Dear old dad," said the soldier, tenderly as a woman, his voice bringing a delicate flush to the old man's cheek, " I'm going to make what men who have served in India call a *bunderbust* with you. I will pay that visit, and will be at least civil enough to Miss Tredethlyn to get some information as to Simon from her, in return for which you'll give me a free hand with the servants. ' Is't a bargain ? ' as your modest McTavish would have it."

"But, my dear boy, you—you wouldn't dis—it would pain me to—— "

" My dear father, the thing's settled. Put

on your hat and coat at once. I'm going to ring for the dog-cart and drive you off to Chillington Vicarage for lunch."

" But—but—my *dear* boy—— "

" I shall call for you again precisely at four o'clock, when we shall proceed to the assault of Moor Gates."

Julius drew his trembling father into the hall, helped him into a light top-coat, placed a stick in his hand, led him out on to the gravel sweep, and fairly started him for the west lodge gate, proposing to pick him up in a few minutes' time.

Immediately afterwards Mr. Children received an order which turned his arrogant heart to water.

" Send my cart round at once; I'm going to drive your master into the town. On my return in thirty minutes you will await me in the billiard-room, with all the other servants, gardeners, grooms, helpers—do you hear ?"

" Yes, sir. Should you wish—— "

"Do you understand my order or not?"

"Yes, sir."

Children withdrew, his florid cheeks paling rapidly.

"It means *the saeck*," he muttered in a sick whisper. "Gawd-forsaken fool that I've been to let slip the best-paid place in the county!"

At the end of half an hour, punctual to the moment, Captain Rush stalked into the billiard-room. In his hand was a heavy riding-whip; his square face was pale, his eyes fierce. As he took up his position upon the hearthrug, facing the little crowd of men and youths, there was dead silence in the room. Not one pair of eyes could meet the captain's: every man present felt that he above all would be singled out for punishment—and that he had well earned it. But a week or two ago a retired non-commissioned officer of his regiment had been discoursing to them of the young master,

declaring him to be one of the tautest cap-
tains in the service. Upon his promotion
from lieutenant to captain, "A" troop, the
rowdiest in the regiment, had been given into
his charge, and for four weeks he had made
the lives of "A" troop a burden. They
used to boast about it afterwards, when they
had learnt to understand him and swear by
him. Briefly, his reputation had a foundation
in solid fact.

This stern captain of dragoons now saw
before him the faces of those who had been
despitefully using the old man for whom he
had a protecting love fathoms deep; whose
very timidity he reverenced; who had never
spoken otherwise than gently to any one of
them; whose lavish kindness they had re-
quited with vulgar scorn. It gave him keen
pleasure to note how cowed and miserable
they looked; nor would he for a time break
a silence which they evidently found so
punishing. But when his words did come

it seemed that the silence must have been full of comfort; he seemed not merely to be speaking, but to be lashing and scourging them with whips. They were ashamed almost to breathe. Yet his language was not violent; he swore not once, but seemed to turn their hearts inside out, and to scorch them through and through. He said things of which the echo would hang about the house for many a long day. When he had finished this strange unconventional address, he dismissed with formal words, Children, the butler, McTavish, Tomlinson, the second footman, and two other delinquents.

Children plucked up courage so far as to say—

"I require a month's warning, sir."

"You require a sound thrashing, sir!" thundered the captain, "and that you'll get if I find you anywhere within the ring-fence of Bickington Park after four o'clock this afternoon."

McTavish also essayed a word or two, but even his overbearing self-confidence had evaporated.

" Ye'll no get anither mon like——" he began, then broke off with a quaver under the captain's gaze.

" Leave my presence at once, you five," proceeded the bitter voice. " Your wages up to this day month will be sent to the butler's pantry. If I find any one of you about the place on my return this afternoon, you know what to expect."

They filed out of the room, glad to get beyond reach of the dagger-tongue.

Then Captain Rush spoke more kindly to the remainder. There were some decent men and lads among them, though as usual the black-sheep had set the tune for the rest of the flock to dance to. They were not to be let off too easily, however, and breathed more freely when the signal to depart was at length given them.

Julius Rush laughed grimly to himself when the billiard-room door closed upon the last man. " The dear old dad," he muttered, thrashing his leg so hard as to mark it for a month, though he felt not a stroke at the time, " the dear old dad will have a spell of peace after this. For once in my life I've done something unconventional. Were servants ever treated like this before, I wonder? Even now have they got their deserts? Anyway I have tasted revenge—and I like the flavour."

But the young master had not quite done with them yet; the practice of revenge seemed to have improved his appetite, though not his temper. He made an excellent luncheon, and was served with obsequious alacrity; yet he complained of everything that was done. Not a soul in the house, man or woman, could move or speak aright. Not content with scarifying them as a body, he now proceeded to rate each one sepa-

rately.   They said the devil had got hold of
the young master ; but they flew to his word
of command.

A kind of mute despair had settled down
upon the entire household by the time the
captain's dog-cart came round ; but no
temper was exhibited.   His fury had obliterated all that, as a thunder-shower the
sprinkling of a child's watering-can.

Julius would have no man with him, for
he was tired of his own wrath, and wished to
relax unseen.   It was not easy to quiet
himself down, however, his whole system
being so charged with indignation ; and as
he trotted gently between flower-trimmed
hedges, and amid the merry flutings of the
blackbirds, little spurts of vicious laughter
cleft the scent-laden air.   But he was a
strong-willed man, and Nature was doing
her best to ease him of his humours.

Mr. Rush was almost afraid to look at his
son when the cart drew up at the vicarage,

but Julius had got himself in hand by then, and was as gentle as a woman with his old father; so calm and serene, indeed, as to make it clear that he had done nothing very terrible.

"Well, Julius," said the squire, a little nervously, as they were mounting the station hill, "I see by your manner that—that you have let those poor fellows off easily?"

"Too easily by half; but that's a forbidden topic. What you have to do, my dear father, is to drink in the sunshine and brace yourself to face Miss Tredethlyn— whom I hate less than I did this morning."

Had Julius allowed his father to guess how deep a tragedy had been enacting at home, he knew that the old man would have been positively incapable of facing Kate for a day or two. Instead of which, he cheered and encouraged him by such little devices as a mother might have used to hearten up a shy young girl, so that when the moment arrived the squire was able to inquire for Miss Tredethlyn with hardly a tremor in his voice.

Some painful seconds ensued, however, for Miss Tredethlyn was having tea in the garden with a friend ; and the friend, as they at once perceived on emerging from the house, was Mrs. French-Chichester. During the short walk across the shadow-dappled lawn, the squire's courage lapsed away, leaving him a mere bundle of nerves, for the gentle old man had been a good deal shaken by domestic worries lately, and dreaded the popular widow even more than Miss Tredethlyn.

Fortunately it happened that Mrs. French-Chichester had risen to depart, and only stayed long enough to tease Mr. Rush by a few questions on subjects about which he was painfully conscious of his own ignorance. True, in those few minutes she contrived to make the old man wretched, the dragoon

furious, and her hostess miserably uncom-
fortable; but she thereupon shook hands
with all three most cordially, and departed,
wreathed in smiles.

Then followed an awkward pause, broken
only by a remark or two upon the blossom-
laden horse-chestnut under which they were
sitting.

Kate had been supporting her friend's
stinging condolences with the kind of stoicism
which is apt to end hysterically, and even in
a happier mood would have been deeply
embarrassed at receiving these two — the
tailor whom she had openly scorned, the
tailor's son whom she, the gin-distiller's
granddaughter, had snubbed so haughtily.
Had they come to triumph over her she
could have faced them without flinching;
but she was as clearly conscious of the old
gentleman's kindly motives as though he
had expounded them for an hour. In truth,
she felt more like crying than making con-

versation, and Captain Rush perceived that the visit would be the dead failure he had expected.

Mr. Rush, after straining his mind almost to the cracking-point for a topic, hazarded an inquiry after Kate's father.

Mr. Tredethlyn was still at Lymport. He had written a letter which, while easing his own mind, had been to Kate's as a tight boot to a tender foot. From the safe vantage-ground of the Royal Hotel he could express himself with a frankness impossible with less than forty miles between himself and Kate; and there was a peculiar charm in thus pouring forth home-truths from a safe distance upon one who was apt to have the best of it in close encounters.

The letter set forth how, from sheer tenderness towards Kate's most obvious weakness, her father had withheld the truth as to her mother's humble origin. Priding herself as she had done almost from childhood upon her superiority to some nine-tenths of her neighbours, it would have been, he conceived, little short of brutal to humiliate her without adequate cause. Now that she knew the worst, she must bear it as best she could. Nell had been in possession of the secret for years, but she was cast, if he might be forgiven for saying so, in a nobler mould than her sister. And let Kate remember that all the comforts and luxuries of her life sprang from this much-despised trade. But for that, she must needs have been a poor parson's daughter, bound down to some paltry country village, immersed in mean economies, sighing in vain for decent society. Her father's old Cornish pedigree would have been but a poor solace under the burden of such an environment. Again, his motives in marrying out of his caste had been of the highest, and so on, and so on.

A good deal of the letter was true; and all of it was bitter to its recipient. Mr.

Tredethlyn had concluded his not uncongenial task by stating flatly that he had no intention of returning home until Kate should be ready to receive him in a fitting spirit, and refrain from harping upon topics calculated to produce discord in a comfortable home.

It happened that this letter of parental admonition was now to fulfil a purpose quite outside its writer's intentions.

For Kate was in the peculiar wrought-up condition in which a person's real emotional self is apt to burst forth in unexpected fashion. Her wrath against her father had been boiling over for these four days, but anger was now streaked with the self-reproach of a woman generous at the core, and so moved to over-estimate the enormity of her own pettiness. She had been taking herself severely to task for past misconduct to the tailor, and now here was the tailor in person, shaming her with fresh kindness ;

for his delicate respect and sympathy were perfectly visible through the awkwardness of his manner.

Captain Rush, who was observing her with a certain grim coolness, saw something — as much as a member of the blinder sex could be expected to see—of what was passing in her mind, but was far from prepared for what came next; indeed, a sudden fall of snow through the June sunshine might well have amazed him less; for Kate turned upon the old squire—over whose head she had been looking for some years—her clear strong gaze, drew from her pocket her father's stinging letter, and read out to him the portions in which her own failings were handled.

The old man blushed as warmly as herself the while, and looked far more horrified.

" My dear," he said, shakily rising, hat in hand, while a snow of delicate chestnut petals fluttered down upon his grey head—

"my dear—if you'll forgive an old man calling you so just this once—I can't abear to see you vex yourself so ; my respect for you is more hearty than ever it was afore. I can't express myself as I should like, but do put up the letter, there's a dear. I do think your father's very 'ard—I should say hard—upon you ; and—and I'm a'most too flustered to say anythink else."

Kate folded the letter up as steadily as she could, and resumed her seat.

There was to be no more demonstration, though there is no knowing to what sentimental length the pair might have gone but for the presence of a critical third person.

No sign came from Captain Rush, but his heart danced for a moment or two. He admitted to himself that Kate had done well ; that the reading of this indictment against herself amounted to a full apology for past rudeness to his father. But, though she had risen in his esteem, his sullen pride was yet far from the melting point. He could be good friends with Kate in future, but would lower himself no more by the offer of unacceptable homage.

Wishing to brace up the pair and give a lighter tone to the conversation, he offered to give them an account of his dealings with the servants at Bickington.

Mr. Rush listened to the curt narrative, holding fast to his chair, palpitating with excitement, his face a moving picture of horror and admiration, dread and relief. "How terribly hard of you," he seemed to say, "yet how bold! How terrifying, yet infinitely comforting!" Presently terror mastered the other feelings.

"But, my dear son," he murmured shakily, "how shall I face them now?"

"There'll be none to face. The five whom I dismissed will be out of sight before we return."

"D—do you think so?"

" I know it," said Julius, grimly.

" They have only got their deserts," cried Kate, eagerly ; " and I wish I had been there to see justice done upon them." Her eyes and the captain's flashed together for a moment, then parted slowly.

The squire's terror died gradually but surely. There ensued a relief deep as an ocean, calm as a sleeping infant. The rich beauty of the opening summer seemed to emerge for him as from a veil withdrawn. He leaned back and drank in the world of sun and blossom, murmuring—

" Children gone, and McTavish—never to return ! "

" Never, dear old dad," muttered Julius ; and perhaps he and Kate were also inclined to detect subtle beauties where mere grass and flowers had been. At any rate, they began to talk to each other, while the squire listened in luxurious silence, and thought the millennium had come.

Captain Rush explained how anxious he was to see Simon ; how his father had made one or two more efforts to do so, and been rebuffed ; how his own letters had remained unanswered. Did Miss Tredethlyn think there was any hope of getting at his friend ? Could she tell him anything as to Simon's plans and intentions ?

Kate, being the only person whom Simon ever received as a visitor, could answer most questions about him ; indeed, it was no small relief to be able to discuss Simon and his situation with those who cared for him, instead of proclaiming his innocence to deaf ears.

"I shall be glad to talk of him," she said, turning her eyes towards the Hollacomb vale, a glimpse of which was visible through the lilacs, "though it is rather a mournful subject. Poor old Simon ! You wouldn't be surprised at his neglect of your letters, Captain Rush, if you could get a glimpse of him now. He is changed—so soured and broken-spirited and cynical that you would hardly know him. I fear he deserves his nickname now. 'Timon of Chillington' he has become in very truth."

Kate then told them, with an unusual thrill in her voice, the story already known to the reader of Joyce's death, and of her charge to Simon.

"This sad business," she proceeded, "was of some service to Simon. The responsibility of the child's guardianship is good for him, and the mother's pathetic circumstances rekindled an old idea in his mind. Among his hundred schemes you may have heard him speak of that of founding a hospital for the dying. Such a thing has been discussed in the magazines and public journals, and the stories told of working girls and women overtaken by disease, and hiring garrets in which to die, took a deep hold of Simon. The hospital was to have been a great undertaking, properly organized and equipped, but his many failures have humbled poor old Simon. He told me that he had no spirit for another big failure; but wishing to make one last experiment before leaving the country for good, he proposed to turn Hollacomb Farm into a small hospital for homeless people to die in, surrounded at least with decent care and moderate comfort. Of course I encouraged him—and now the thing's done, as you know, Mr. Rush."

"Yes, I've heard about it, Miss Kate, but should like to hear more; and nearly all this is news to my son."

"Well, he has arranged for four beds, and a trained nurse, and Mr. Syme is the medical attendant, and there's really little more to tell. The thing is all on a small scale, but quite a success at present. The patients have shown themselves grateful to Simon; and little Rose makes the dying people smile as she patters in and out of the rooms. The woods look beautiful now, and sometimes the poor things are carried out beside the canal, as if to take a last farewell of trees and flowers and sunshine; and altogether there's a strange beauty and pathos, as of mournful music, about the place—and I don't know that I care to talk about it any more."

For a moment or two the white blossoms fell upon a silent party; then Kate resumed, turning abruptly to Captain Rush with the air of one resolved not to shirk a painful topic.

"I hope you side with me against Simon's accusers?"

"My mind is dark upon that question," he answered slowly. "I can't believe what they say, yet know now how to disbelieve it thoroughly."

"He's the last man in God's universe to wrong a poor girl and leave her to destroy herself," said the old man, solemnly; "and

I feel in my heart that the Almighty will one day see the innocent righted and the guilty punished."

Kate looked wistful, but full of doubt. Julius Rush looked bitter and sceptical.

" The world's a seething mass of innocent suffering," he muttered.

" If I were but a man—— " began Kate, impulsively.

" What could you do ? " the soldier retorted with asperity. " What could you do for a man who won't even assert his own innocence ? who won't see a friend ? won't answer a friend's letters ? "

" Fight for him behind his back—fight tooth and nail to see him righted—that's what I could do. And can you wonder at his hopeless kind of silence when every one condemns him, even his own father and his once-friend Terence ; even my sister, who I did think knew him better ? Were I a man," she continued, with kindling eyes and a contemptuous glance at the one who seemed so lukewarm in a friend's cause, " I would labour and strive, and ransack and delve and rummage till I had plucked out the heart of this mystery, and removed the blot upon the honour of one whom I believe to be nothing short of a hero."

Rush still looked unmoved ; seemingly he refused to be inoculated with Kate's ardour. Perhaps he took a perverse pleasure in not showing his better side, perhaps was minded to prolong an indignant outburst which pleased him ; at any rate, his face was inscrutable. His cool, unimpressed attitude certainly incited Kate to fresh efforts. She waxed sarcastic as well as warm.

" Sometimes," she resumed, " I'm inclined to think, with Mrs. French-Chichester, that man is literally all self, a creature bound to his own *ego* as to a post, and railed round with iron spikes of self-interest. I speak to my father of Simon, and he shrugs his shoulders without a word ; to the vicar, and he looks blank as a wall and fetches a hopeless sigh ; to Terence, and he changes the subject with an angry jerk of his head."

" But my son has been away all these months," urged Mr. Rush, anxiously.

" I'm talking generalities," snapped Kate.

" Rather particular generalities," the captain remarked drily.

" I shall be more particular directly. I say it's a shame, a burning shame, that no hand should be raised to help Simon. He'll leave the country soon for good—for I know his plans—drift away into the world without a spoken regret to follow him, without a soul to care whether he lives or dies."

" I fear it will be so," sighed Mr. Rush, "though already there's a feeble sort of reaction in his favour. Many a time have I heard 'em jeer at his schemes and hobbies, and explain away his merits, as people are so clever at doing.   But I do think this last matter of the hospital has set 'em wondering a bit ; and they do speak kind of him here and there just now."

"Oh yes," quoth Kate ; "most people keep a little justice and charity locked up somewhere in chests and drawers, and offer us a spoonful or two when the struggle's over and we need it no more.   Why, we may look for kindness even, once we're past using it !"

"I'm bound to say, however "—the exasperating captain seemed bent upon trying Kate's temper to the utmost—"that Simon has not yet given his public a chance of unlocking the chests and drawers you were speaking of."

Kate glared at the speaker and relapsed into silence.   Mr. Rush murmured something deprecating at his son, but was quenched by a single glance.

Julius proceeded with an unruffled front

and the assurance of one who is complete master of the field.

"And now, Miss Tredethlyn, as I have listened to your strictures with some patience, you will perhaps allow me to explain that I had, even before coming here, made a resolution to undertake the quest which you have urged upon me with such eloquence—indeed, that the object of our visit was simply the gaining of information that might further that undertaking. I *intend* to penetrate the mystery, and shall give all my spare time to the quest until some solution can be arrived at. But I believe that to rush at it in an impulsive feminine sort of way would be to court failure."

Kate still wore a frown; but a smile might be read between the lines of it.

"Why didn't you say so before?" she asked, the fire in her eyes still smouldering.

He made no answer, though his square chin seemed to say, "You never gave me a chance!"

" May I ask what your plan of campaign may be, Captain Rush ? "

" In the first place, I propose to employ a private detective. Has that intention your approval ? "

" Certainly not. This is not a case for a mere common professional man ; it needs sympathetic insight of a special character to penetrate the motives of a man like Simon."

" I'm sorry you don't approve ; but I shall try the detective."

" When he has failed," said Kate, icily, " perhaps you will again come to me for advice."

" Very likely. What would you in that case suggest ? "

" I should say, go and consult Ezekiel Doidge. That man cares more than any living person about finding out the truth of the matter ; and he has in his possession all the trinkets, letters, and such things of his dead sweetheart. He is shrewd, too, and keen as a sleuth-hound. I believe you and Mr. Doidge together might delve out the heart of the mystery. You might right Simon in the face of all men, restore him to his father, save for him his patrimony, which now stands to be thrown to the dogs or handed over to public charities; and so might earn the deep gratitude of the one or two friends that he has left in the world."

"I'm glad you're hopeful, but shall try my own plan first."

"I don't doubt that for an instant. And the plan will fail."

"Not until it has had a fair trial, however."

Captain Rush then turned to his father and suggested that it was time to be going; and the squire, of course, rose obediently to the hint. Miss Tredethlyn and Julius then exchanged a final defiant glance, and the party broke up, the squire carrying with him a treasure in the shape of a new and piquant sensation. Kate had warmly pressed his hand.

CHAPTER III.

WHAT of Terence Clancy since we saw him some months ago? He has enjoyed good health, and, at least to the superficial observer, such an average allowance of happiness as every man who has not actually committed a murder considers his due. His practice grows and flourishes; his popularity, so far from being on the wane, has deepened and widened. He esteems and reverence his wife more than ever, and still loves her a good deal. Yet Terence has still a reserve fund of unsatisfied desires, and is in possession of several pegs good enough to hang self-pity upon.

His beautiful wife, for instance, is from
one point of view a somewhat costly possession, involving the maintenance of a high
moral level of daily life, the breathing of an
ethical atmosphere too fine for perfect
comfort. What his nature really demands
of woman is a smooth caressing tolerance,
a sympathetic acceptance of the bad in him
as well as the good, a tender worship of
Terence Clancy as he stands. Now Nell
has measured him for a hero, and her
insistently high opinion of him seems to
hang upon him like the proverbial giant's
robe ; insomuch that it is a relief sometimes
to get among inferior women, with no
troublesome ideal to be lived up to.

Even in his professional rounds he feels
that Nell's eye is upon him. She is always
keeping him up to the mark, always thinking
of how to clear off that tiresome debt to
Simon. Yet she never nags or harasses
him, and he freely admits to himself that,

without her constant encouragement, he would before now have sunk into abject idleness.   For Terence hates work, and knows that he does.   The drudgery of his profession sits so heavily upon him that at times he has it in him to sell the practice and live in a cottage on the proceeds.

Such minor troubles seem to call for attention first as being the most insistent, and those most often discussed with a man's self.   But of the deeper pains that gnaw silently, and cling miasma-like about the secret parts of the soul, Terence has some knowledge.

Here, again, Nell is in a measure to blame.   With a wife of lower moral calibre his conscience would not be so uneasy ; but Nell is like a fire near which self-comforting sophistry shrivels up and dies.   To be happy with a woman of an honesty so rigid, of so crystal-clear a conscience, he should either be a much better man or a much worse ; either as spotless as herself, or free enough from virtuous prejudice to despise her ideal and laugh over it in secret. As it is, what might have been but a speck upon his consciousness is an ugly blotch which time fails to erase. His sin of treachery to Simon is not "ever before him," but it underlies other things and crops up just when he looks for peace.

But, confession being a thing that he has ceased even to contemplate as a possibility, there remains to Terence nothing but the weak man's anodyne—compromise. He is aware that public opinion is softening towards Simon, and can afford to take comfort from that knowledge. For he has little to fear on his own account now—the hue and cry being practically over—and in time people will doubtless come to forgive the supposed culprit and allow his many good deeds to counterpoise that one bad slip. As to Sir Hamo, Terence fully intends to bring about a reconciliation between him and Simon. He means to change his own views gradually, to become after a time doubtful as to Simon's guilt, to lead the old man along the groove of this changed attitude until he shall be ready to take back his son into favour.

As Terence and his wife are now so frequently at the hall, sometimes living there for several weeks in succession, this plan seems the more feasible. Meanwhile Sir Hamo's romantic affection for Nell grows, rather than diminishes, with declining health —a state of things that no one perceives more clearly than Mrs. French-Chichester. She begins to perceive that all her pains will probably result in the substitution of Nell Clancy in the place of Kathleen French-Chichester as successor to Simon the prodigal. Other shrewd observers, too, are speculating as to the outcome of Sir Hamo's fatherly love, hinting slyly that Clancy is playing his cards well. But herein their shrewdness was much astray, for mercenary calculations had no place among Terence's faults; and the prospect of seeing Nell enriched at Simon's expense, had it occurred to him at all, would only have increased his existing mental harassments.

And one thing more must be touched upon—for now we are upon the subject of that somewhat shattered thing, poor Terence's conscience, it were well to make a clean breast—there is yet another secret weighing upon the man, and this one pricks the sharper for being of a professional nature.

For, if somewhat false and fickle in other relations, Terence has been hitherto without blemish professionally—or had been up to the time of Doidge's denunciation of Simon. From the small frauds and trickeries practised by medical men of crooked tendencies he had kept free ; in fact, to do him full justice, had been a perfectly honest doctor. But in respect of this one patient, Ezekiel Doidge, there was now deep unrest in his mind.

His physical examination of Doidge on the night before the cricket-club meeting had exercised Terence's diagnosing faculty severely. There had been no actual revelation, such as would compel him at once to take action or to give up calling himself an honest man; but certain subtle indications, meaningless to a man of ordinary ability, though to his analytical sense suggestive of the presence of a mortal disease. He had, of course, intended to examine the patient further when opportunity should arise, but his dread of being brought into contact with Ezekiel had resulted in procrastination.

Meanwhile he sopped his conscience by causing his assistant, Jack Syme, to put the patient through a searching examination; which resulted, however, simply in a verdict of general nervous debility.

So far, well; but since then, possibly owing to Nell's unconscious influence, Terence's better self had been worrying him somewhat in the following fashion: "Syme has but commonplace ability; you might almost as well have handed over your patient to a solicitor or a parson; and you never gave Syme the key of your suspicion, you never once breathed the word 'aneurism.' You ought to investigate the case yourself without delay. If the man has an aortic aneurism it will, unless properly treated, grow steadily; one day it will burst, and he'll fall dead in a heap. How will you feel about it then, Terence Clancy? You should at once take steps to verify your suspicions; if they hold good he should be laid on his back, kept from all excitement, dosed with iodide, treated like cracked china."

Upon this aneurism, or enlargement of a great blood-vessel, Terence's mind kept running; but still he took no step beyond the construction, and subsequent demolition, of a whole series of good resolutions. To make up his mind to see Doidge was a nightly task, to escape the task through pressure of other business a daily achievement. But the mental perturbation increased, while his fear of Ezekiel lessened. There came a day, some two weeks after Julius Rush's entry upon the new quest, when Terence had knit himself up to the requisite pitch, and was actually on his way to the mill, proposing to consult Doidge upon some question of the Angling Association, then in course of conversation to speak of his health, and so work his way on by degrees to the needful examination.

Terence found it quite a journey to Doidge's mill, which lay but a short distance above the town. He walked rapidly as far as the town bridge, but at that point his ardour slackened. He began to think of other patients having claims upon his prompt

attention.; his will began to ooze away as
though his mind had sprung a leak somewhere. Fingers seemed to beckon him
north, south, and west, while every fibre of
him shrank from the eastward road. But
Nell, who had unknowingly driven him
hither, urged him to fresh effort ; the thought
of returning to her with one stain washed
from his conscience stiffened the yielding
will. He walked on again, stopping here
and there, pausing and loitering, but not
once turning back.

Now at length he was past the cemetery ;
now had reached the second bridge over the
Chilling, and the murmur of the stream was
full of depression for him. The mill was
now barely fifty yards distant ; the hum and
beat of its machinery were even more dis-
tasteful than the noise of the river.

There was nothing picturesque about
Doidge's flour-mill. It consisted of a group
of new stone buildings, placed astride the

Chilling, and having a physiognomy suggestive of business energy and solid success. Above the roofs towered a tall brick chimney, for Doidge used steam as well as water-power; many wheels were plashing, many stones grinding; whitened men were working busily; clerks coming to and from the office; carts piled with sacks passing in and out of the spacious yard.

As Clancy entered this yard the busy work-a-day aspect of the place impressed him in a wholesome fashion, for in so bustling and cheerful scene there was nothing for morbid fear to fasten upon. Strolling into the office for a moment or two, he further steadied his nerves by a little gossip with Doidge's foreman; and thereafter marched through the flower-garden to the miller's front door with a better head of courage than he had been able to muster since leaving the town bridge.

"Yes, Mr. Doidge was at home, but

engaged"—Terence's heart leaped—"yet doubtless he would see Dr. Clancy"—the heart sank again.

Terence was conducted down a long passage into a small wainscoted parlour, the miller's favourite sitting-room. Its one window looked out upon a breadth of meadow land, cattle-trimmed, intersected by the shining river; and all the land visible from the armchair by the window was Ezekiel's own. Thence he could watch a long reach of the stream, issuing forth occasionally to pounce upon any ticketless stranger whose rod might be seen waving on either bank.

Doidge was seated here to-day, but with his back to the light, and never a thought going poacher-wards.

He rose eagerly to greet Terence, his eyes gleaming, his hands and limbs jerking nervously. Seated at the table, with a cigar between his teeth, was Captain Julius Rush.

Clancy drew a deep breath of relief; for though conscious that Rush disliked him heartily, he was ready to greet as a friend in need any one who should make the dreaded *tête-à-tête* impossible.

The slightest of greetings passed between the dragoon and the doctor; then the latter seated himself hastily, and, with the air of one who has not a moment to spare, put a question to Doidge bearing upon certain rights of the Angling Association.

The miller waved the question aside impatiently—

"Can't talk about that nonsense now, doctor; we've got somethin' a deal more important in hand. Captain,"—he turned abruptly to his other guest,—"I move we take Dr. Clancy into our confidence?"

Captain Rush shook his head and threw one leg over the other impatiently; but Doidge was wont to follow his own wishes, while regarding those of other people as whims. Accordingly, he remained upon his feet, and emphasizing each sentence with his restless hand, began to explain why Captain Rush had come to see him, and how vigorously he was about to plunge into Captain Rush's quest.

The latter, having now no choice as to making a confidant of Clancy, and perhaps expecting to get one or two useful hints· from him, detailed to both listeners the steps he had already taken. He had begun by getting a private detective down from town, equipping him with such information as he possessed, and setting him to work in a business-like fashion; and, after ten days of careful investigation, the infallible professional had this morning delivered his report and verdict—to the effect that the case was clear as day, that Mr. Secretan was without a shadow of doubt the guilty party.

"The numbskull!" cried Ezekiel, with a

stamp; "the addle-pated fool! Just what a d—d professional idiot like that would say!"

"Then you agree with my father and myself?" asked Rush. "I quite expected to find a difficulty in bringing you round to our view of the question."

"Look here!" cried the miller in a blaze of excitement, "first I'm going to swear you both to secrecy, then I shall be free to put you up to a thing or two . . . God's truth, what ails you, sir? You'm as white as a sheet?"

"Rather faint," muttered Clancy, shakily; "throw up the window, will you? I had a bad cropper on the last day of the hunting season—you'll remember it, Rush?—and I've been liable to go faint like this ever since. I'm half afraid there's some internal injury."

"Lord, Lord, and I've never so much as offered you a drink!" Doidge hastily drew a decanter of whisky and some glasses from the cupboard. "Come, have a liquor, doctor; 'tis fine old whisky, and will straighten you up in no time. Captain, have a glass, sir, and pardon my forgetfulness. Damme, sirs, let us drink success to the new chase! I reckon us'll kill afore the month's out. Come, fill up, Doctor Clancy. Here's to a hot scent and a fast run!"

Terence filled with his back to the others. The strong draught brought the blood back to his cheeks, his spirits began to rise. He felt now as a man with back to wall and face to foe; to fight had at last become easier than to run away. His brain had become intensely clear, every nerve was now on the alert; he had never realized until this moment his own power and skill and cunning. He felt this sickly hysterical·enemy to be as a mere child in his hands; he perceived, too, the enormous advantage to himself of thus being called to a seat at the enemy's council board, of knowing every hostile move before it could be put into execution. Surely the veriest fool, with such odds in his favour, might expect to nonplus them ! He drank again, and turned genially to his host.

"Grand whisky, this, Mr. Doidge. You dispense a medicine worth more than my whole drug-shop put together. I'm right as a trivet again already; let us hear what you were going to say."

"I'm to understand clearly that I have your promise of secrecy ? That you'll both keep fast hold o' your tongues until such time as I loose 'em ?"

The soldier nodded gravely. The doctor cried boisterously—

"Ay, ay, fire away, man ; don't kill us with suspense !"

"Then, harkee, you two"—Doidge bent forward, fixing upon them eyes brilliant with excitement—"I've been hunting false all along. Mr. Secretan had nothin' to do with my poor girl's trouble; never made love to her; had no hand whatever in bringing about her death."

"Ah!" murmured the captain, with a deep sigh of satisfaction.

"How do you know that?" asked Clancy, in a dry sceptical voice.

Doidge detailed hurriedly how he had tracked Simon, been on the point of shooting him, and in the nick of time had learned the truth from Joyce's words.

Terence paled again. The picture of this crazed fellow dogging his enemy night after night, gun in hand, filled him with a creeping sickness. He drank again, and took a fresh grip of his courage.

"He's a fool, a crazy monomaniac," he kept repeating to himself. "I shall outwit him to a certainty."

"Yes," concluded the miller, "I had my finger crooked on the trigger; 'twas Joyce that saved his life."

" But suppose he had hoodwinked the woman ? "

" Impossible, doctor. Joyce was Mary's bosom friend, and in all her secrets. It wan't Secretan, I tell you. Joyce's voice bored the fact of his innocence right into me. He's blameless as I am—more so, for he watched over her, while I never stirred a finger to save her."

" In that case," interposed Rush, " I must trouble you to proclaim my friend's innocence at once. He has borne another man's blame long enough."

" Lookee, captain, you'm a bit simpler than I thought. Can't you see that by keeping up that fiction we lull the real man into seeming security—that Mr. Secretan's supposed guilt is a ready-made stalking horse for we ? "

" I can see," retorted the captain, stormfully, " that it's a cursed shame to let him live another day uncleared, and, what's more, I won't permit such a thing ! "

"I don't care about you, or your friend, or any one else. I don't care who suffers, or what happens, or whether I live or die, so I find out Mary's murderer!"

"I'll force you to clear Secretan!"

"I have your promise," shouted Doidge, cursing furiously. "You'm no gentleman, no man, if you go back on your word; you'm a cur even to talk of betrayin' me!"

Here was a brave beginning; with his enemies knocking their heads together thus, Terence might well afford to grow hopeful.

"I decline further speech with you. Go your own way and I'll go mine. You're no better than a madman. I must have broken with you anyway, for I see you mean murder. I'll have none of that. I'll have a curb put on you somehow."

Captain Rush arose, clutching his hat and stick, and regarding poor Doidge with angry contempt. Terence already felt that the plot had collapsed, that he himself would be

the miller's sole coadjutor; but this hopeful
conclusion was a thought too hasty, the
danger was not yet over.

For as Ezekiel, swelling and scowling
with indignation, stood watching the captain's
exit, he put forth his hand to grasp the
table, and touched a writing-desk which had
been lying there since the beginning of the
interview.   He looked down at the desk,
and his face changed.

"Don't go, sir," he muttered brokenly.
"Lord forgive me for helpin' to spoil my
poor girl's chance! Stand by me, sir, even
though I be a hot-tongued fool. I ain't fit
to hunt the man down alone; my strength
has been failin' these months; and—and I
can't do nothin' without help, nowadays.
Don't be afeard that I mean any violence;
I tried that tack once and found I had no
stomach for't; too much of a coward for
that, now my health's gone—too much broke
and wore out and shattered, I reckon!

There's a Bible yonder ; I'll take my oath on't, if you like."

" What is your intention, then ? I don't move a step with you till I know that, Doidge."

" To track him down," said Ezekiel, solemnly laying his hand upon the desk ; " to spend every bit o' health and energy left me, and every farthin' I possess, in findin' him out and bringin' ruin on him."

" I have your solemn promise to drop all thought of violence ? "

" You have, sir. An' for my poor girl's sake stand by a poor devil who han't more than a year or two left to work in."

" You're not fit for this strain and excitement, Doidge," the doctor interposed. " I warn you distinctly that you're shortening your life by going on thus. Give up this insane pursuit and lead a quiet life, taking care never to overtask or over-excite yourself, and your health may be restored."

"I'm cool enough now," said Ezekiel, "and I shan't break out again. I'm gettin' hopeful, and that does me good. With the help o' you two I'll get through this job; after which I don't care what comes to me. Look here, sir "—he turned to Captain Rush as the latter resumed his seat—"you can guess what things I have put away in this desk ? "

The soldier nodded gravely. Terence shuddered and palpitated. The faintness was coming over him again, and the worst moment was yet to be faced. He knew not what relics of poor Mary's dead romance were to be laid before him. No thinkable ordeal could have been more painful to him than this that was coming. Even Doidge himself, had he known all, could hardly have devised for his enemy a sharper punishment. He had to bend over the desk with the others, but contrived to stand behind them, leaning heavily upon a corner of the table, and once more the extremity of his danger was fortifying.

The soldier looked down with sympathy and interest as Doidge unlocked the desk and threw back the cover. Ezekiel himself seemed transformed for the moment; his animal passions seemed to fall away, as though he were in the actual presence of his dead love; his hand strayed forward as a mother's towards a sleeping child.

He first drew forth a ring, a dainty little thing set with a single pearl of small value.

Terence felt the sting of tears in his eyes; he remembered Mary's humble joy on receiving the trinket, how she had kissed it and cried over it, and been silent for an hour after he had placed it on her finger. Almost he had it in him to cry aloud, "The culprit stands here before you. Do your worst; for you can't hate him more bitterly than he hates himself!"

But when the miller handed to Captain

Rush a copy of Moore's " Melodies," Terence's remorseful longing was at once obliterated by fear. There would be his own handwriting to greet him from the title-page. He turned away for one insupportable moment.

" Title-page torn out," remarked Rush, grimly ; " evidently the poor girl has spared no pains to baffle us. Nothing but a few marks and annotations in pencil—all half erased. This book will not advance us an inch upon our way. Have you no letters or notes, or even a single line in the man's handwriting ? "

" Not a line," sighed Doidge.

Under this new encouragement Terence's crushed spirit uprose ; he was able to handle the relics—one or two more books, some dried forget-me-nots, and other trifling keepsakes—and to offer a few appropriate comments upon the difficulties of the situation.

There was nothing more to be examined ;

but they sat long discussing a plan of campaign, Terence bearing his part with the others, and skilfully laying false tracks for them whenever an opportunity arose. Under his delicate manipulation they were always kept wide of the true road; but the strain and stress of his position told heavily upon him the while. When they at length separated he felt weak and shattered, and full of gloomy foreboding ; nor was his conscience eased one jot in respect of Ezekiel's physical condition, for he had noted more than one subtle token tending to substantiate his fears—or were they now hopes ?

Slowly and painfully Terence dragged himself up the hill towards the White House, yearning only to throw himself upon Nell's mercy, entreat her to take him out of the miserable net in which he had become entangled, to begin with him a new life in some distant country.

CHAPTER IV.

WHILE Terence was working out at the mill the sentence pronounced upon him by Nemesis, Nell was sitting at home indulging in morbid introspection. This was not a usual failing of hers, but Terence's restless, unsettled condition was beginning to make its mark upon his wife. She had not the comfortable stupidity which blunders cheerfully along, unperceptive of, and consequently unharassed by, any but its own personal cares, nor had she now that absolute trust in Terence which would some months ago have attributed his troubled state to the wear of professional anxieties or other legitimate causes. His disquiet now filled her with a dull pain, for which the routine of household duties was no sufficient antidote.

Towards the end of the forenoon she took her work down to a rustic seat among the shrubs at the bottom of the garden, resolving to ply her needle hard, and leave thinking alone altogether. As well have made up her mind to let breathing alone ; thought but flowed the swifter for being dammed up by will for a brief period.

Nell began to review her life since marriage with a candour she had never before permitted herself. Hitherto self-blame had sufficed when anything had to be explained away, but now reason demanded that Terence, too, should be criticized. It seemed that she must either blame him mildly, or herself grow bitter ; must let the dissatisfied corner of her mind have its say before she could perceive how best to under-take Terence's defence. He still loved and reverenced her. With these grand central facts to support her she could surely afford to consider his little failings with calmness? For instance, let it be frankly admitted that he had a certain tender flirting way with women that often gave her jealous pangs, a certain crying need for the confidence and sympathy of every pretty girl who crossed his path. Well, this was, after all, nothing but an efflorescence of good nature. She ought to take shame to herself for such paltry jealousy.

Again, Terence had a little weakness, which she now touched upon with a quick, pained flush, for small falsehoods — mere blarneyings sometimes, doubtless springing from the same source as the other weakness. She had herself a powerful bias in the direction of strict truth ; but, then, Terence was far more good natured than she, and over-kindness is surely an amiable failing. She had noticed a similar tendency in his

two little brothers, now domiciled at the
White House, and going daily to the best
school in the town. Towards these little
red-headed fellows Nell had played the part
of a true mother, but their trickiness had
somehow diluted the affection she had tried
hard to give them. They were rough, noisy,
and without any of Terence's physical
refinement; indeed, to be perfectly frank,
they were common looking. But, had they
been honest boys, Nell felt that she could
have loved them well.

This kindly moral weakness of her
husband's sometimes produced a dull ache
in Nell's mind, as well as a sense of alarmed
expectation. There were possibilities about
him not hitherto suspected. The mind which
had been to her as an open book was discovered to have dim corners into which
she feared to penetrate. He had certainly
deceived her, or allowed her to glide into
an erroneous impression, as to his people;

for it was clear, from a dozen explanatory trifles let fall by the small brothers, that the Clancys were not exactly the poor gentle-folks pictured to herself and others. Nor would Terence on any account allow her to pay them a visit.

"They are a bit rough at home, dear," he had explained once or twice. "And, you see, I had to blarney you a bit, or maybe you'd never have learned to love me."

This, with a smile and a caress, adjusted the matter perfectly, as he thought, and was very honest and straightforward to boot; but there was a "but" involved here, as in other matters, when viewed with Nell's eyes.

In brief, it will be seen that the denuding forces of real life had been paring down the ideal image of a husband that Nell had set up, as wind, rain, and frost wear away even hard rock. She had resisted the denudation with all the power of a strong, loyal nature, but the figure had been slowly " weathered " nevertheless.

As Nell came to this admission in the course of her thinking, some tears fell upon the work with which her hands were resolutely busy. She perceived, moreover, that there was nothing to be done ; by no conceivable treatment could she infiltrate strict honesty into a character like Terence's. It was like a sieve very suitable for holding ordinary grain, but incapable of retaining the fine gold-dust of absolute truth. Had this disillusion come suddenly she might have despaired ; but so gradual had been the process, that her present task consisted of the mere summing up of previous impressions, and the spreading out of their results for inspection.

Nor was she one to sit still and allow a grievance to ravage her heart and mind at its will, for Nell had the combative spirit that loves not surrender. Having allowed

herself to draw the veil from truth, she
would neither cover it up again nor shrink
from regarding it.   It was clear to her that
she must either readjust her conception of
life, learning to take things and people as
they are, or sink into a state of permanent
morbid depression.   She must, in fact, learn
to take Terence as a whole, together with
all his limitations, to love him in spite of
his failings.   The decision cheered and
strengthened her; and, being unaware that
her relation to Terence was of a kind as old
as the human race, her solution of the difficulty one of the most ordinary and inevitable
in the long history of woman's love, she felt
something of an inventor's triumph.   It
appeared that she had done a clever thing,
as well as the right thing; wherefore her
self-respect was increased, her conscience
satisfied.

When the boys came home from school,
Nell went up the garden to welcome them.

They rushed in, bawling, stamping, and banging doors, but they clung to and caressed her as a mother. To them, at least, she had done her duty straitly, so here again she felt cheered.

Presently she saw them fairly started upon a fishing excursion, heavily victualled, and burning with enthusiasm, and herself returned to the garden with some of their good spirits reflected on her face.

Upon emerging from the bushes she found Terence, somewhat to her surprise, reclining on the garden seat. He must have come in by the lower gate in the wall; and she perceived at once from his attitude that something was wrong with him. He looked harassed and overwrought, and, as he caught sight of his wife, his face took an expression of something like terror.

Nell was almost rejoiced to find him thus with his trouble at the climax point. Now was her opportunity for bold entry upon the new course.   She would force his confidence, as she ought to have done long ago, and inoculate him with her own growing courage. She sat down close beside her husband, laying a slender hand enticingly upon his shoulder.

"What is it, Terence dear ?   Has something upset you ? or is it that you've been overworked lately ?   I know there has been something on your mind, and blame myself for not being more sympathetic and considerate the last few weeks.   You must forgive me, dear, and let me share your troubles, for really, really I'm not so very hard-judging ; at least, I won't be any more."

The young wife looked very sweet and winning as she bent over him with parted lips and eyes full of sympathy ; but her look and touch were too much for Terence in his present state.   What dregs of spirit and courage the trying scene at the mill had left him evaporated, and a gush of profound self-pity overwhelmed him. He sank on his knees beside Nell, buried his head in her lap, and sobbed like a child.

Nell put her arms about his neck, and they wept together, and this miserable moment had a core of strange happiness for them both. The constraint which had been growing between husband and wife was broken down. Nell felt that all his faults were being swept away in the outrush of her pity, that he was all her own, to be cherished and comforted and loved; while he felt that, come what might, she loved him; that this love of a wife, noble and faultless in his eyes, was a thing to lean upon and take refuge in. Could he but keep this, he might hope to bear up against whatsoever shame or disgrace might be in store for him.

"Dearest, tell me your trouble," urged Nell, with courage in her voice as well as tenderness. "Let me bear it with you. Won't you let your own wife help you?"

"I'm miserable, Nell, miserable," he groaned. "There's a bitter enemy seeking to ruin me."

"What can he do? What possible hold can he have upon you? Won't you tell me?"

There was a flutter of Nell's eyes now, but she managed to keep it out of her voice.

"He'll ruin me, Nell! I tell you he has power to do it."

"What is it, Terence? Oh, pray tell me at once!"

"You shrink from me already—I feel that you shrink from me."

"No, I don't shrink; but the suspense tortures me. It would comfort me to know the worst at once."

"Nell, you might hate me if I told you."

"I could never hate you, Terence—I think not, I hope not, I'm sure not!"

"Could you give up a great deal for me?

hold fast to me through—through heavy troubles ? "

" I know that I could," she answered proudly. " If there be any money difficulty, do not hesitate to tell me all. We can give up our house, go into a mere cottage, and work harder. I don't fear poverty ; I only fear lest this wretched secret may eat away our love if you persist in withholding from me your confidence. Tell me all, I entreat you."

"Could you even leave the country with me, and begin life anew in a foreign land ? "

" I could do that and more." Nell's answer came without hesitation ; but her face was getting pale and drawn, she had begun to dread the coming revelation exceedingly.

Terence, feeling how her arms and hands trembled, grew fearful again ; his heart sank lower and lower. The anguish of confessing all was too sharp to be faced, and a half-confession was not possible. He might bring himself to say, "I was Mary Pethick's lover," were it not that this one statement would involve the further admission—"I have let Simon bear my punishment all these months." To the first offence he might plead guilty; to the second, never. Nothing should ever drag from him the admission of his treachery to Simon; he could neither abase himself so low, nor exalt Simon to such a pitch. There was jealousy involved as well as fear; the two together over-mastered him now, and would continue to do so to the end of the chapter. His fit of despair was passing, too. The mere giving way to his emotions and outpouring of his heaviness had given him relief; a sanguine streak was already illumining his depression. He began to perceive that he had too readily given way to panic and pessimism. What danger worthy of all this fright was attachable to a few faded flowers and a book with half-erased annotations? The sight of the ring had scared him most, but he began to reflect now upon the extreme improbability of its leading to any discovery. He had bought it at a small jeweller's shop, buried in the most crowded part of Lymport, a great seaport town. He was a perfect stranger to the shopman, had paid in gold for the ring without even mentioning his name; he had scarcely been in the shop five minutes. Tush! conscience should make a puling coward of him no longer.

But this same cowardice had already landed Terence in a dilemma. How was he to satisfy this anxious wife of his? He remained with his face buried in her lap, thinking how to solve the new problem.

Meanwhile the suspense was telling upon Nell. His talk of leaving the country was full of alarming suggestion. Was he about to confess some crime? Was her affection, already somewhat bruised and strained, to be put to some insupportable test?

"Nell!"

"Yes, dear." Her voice trembled now, and her breath came short; his long silence had made self-control very difficult.

"Have I frightened you, little Nell?"

"A little, Terence."

"Sure I was always a morbid fool, Nellie; given to take things hardly, to make a mountain out of every molehill of worry. You were right as to my being overworked, and I suppose I must take a holiday soon. I've been worrying a great deal lately, as you know—it has been about a case, dear."

"Tell me about it; to talk over the trouble will be a relief to us both."

"Yes, yes, it will. I'll tell you all about it, though, of course, there's no need to mention the man's name. The long and short of it is that I've made a bad blunder in diagnosis—a most unusual thing with me, little Nell, for I'm rather strong in that direction. A patient came to me some time ago with what I now believe to be an aneurism, or swelling of a great blood-vessel ; a dangerous, probably incurable, trouble. I failed to perceive this, assumed him to be suffering only from general debility, and so the mischief has been allowed to grow unchecked. My error is likely to cost the man his life, do you see ? "

" I am listening, Terence."

" This blunder will be a slur upon my professional skill ; it may cost me ever so many patients, may go far towards ruining my practice and reducing us to downright poverty. You don't seem to appreciate how serious are the probable consequences of this slip of mine ? "

" I'm listening to all you say."

" I do wish you'd be more sympathetic, Nell. You don't understand how painful to a man of any ability the discovery of such a blunder must be ! And my enemies are certain to make the most of it. I say it may cost me my practice, and I can't face the thought of plunging a beloved wife into poverty without pain and horror. Surely you must see that 'tis yourself I'm so anxious about ? "

Terence was now seated beside his wife, looking uneasily at her downcast face. There was something vexatious, if not alarming, about her wooden reception of this explanation. He was telling the literal truth—or, at least, but a slightly modified version of it—and his manner of narration was so consummately natural as almost to impose upon himself. He had almost persuaded himself into the belief that the aneurism was really his central trouble just now. How could she fail to be properly impressed by his plain statement ?

" Have you nothing to say, Nell ? " His tone was that of a man somewhat hurt, but too considerate of her to make any complaint.

If Nell had anything to say she was

unable to get the words out. She wanted
to put several questions; to ask, "Who are
your enemies? How could a mere error in
judgment like that cause in you the terror
and despair which I noticed but a few
minutes ago?"

But she was sick at heart, and in need of
all her powers for the difficult task of self-
persuasion. She had to believe what he
said, was resolutely setting her mind to do
so; but to accomplish this task it was first
needful to crush a powerful sceptical instinct.
Terence's face wore the deprecating, feminine
kind of smile that she had learnt to associate
with tarradiddles, small or great.

Her looks remaining troubled, her eyes
declining to meet his, Terence's smile faded.
He took her hand and kissed it with mournful tenderness. She evidently misunderstood
him, his manner seemed to say, but nothing
could ever abate his chivalrous affection for
her.

Nell was miserable at her inability to respond to his caress, and yearned the more to be convinced.

"What steps do you now intend to take?" she asked timidly.

"I'm going to see Jack Syme about it now, tell him my views, and send him to see the man to-morrow. Jack has seen him once already, and fallen into the same mistake as myself; but there are fresh symptoms now, and I have little doubt but that he will agree with my present view of the case."

"But—but why not go yourself, Terence?"

"It is especially necessary not to alarm or excite the patient, and I think that danger will be lessened if I only send my assistant. I shall afterwards confer with Jack, and the patient will be treated entirely under my direction."

Terence had now really made up his mind to impart his views to his assistant, and set him to work to minutely examine Ezekiel.

He was greatly relieved at the thought of thus shifting the responsibility over to Jack's shoulders ; for now, were Ezekiel in course of time to die of this aneurism, surely he, Terence, need feel no qualm of conscience in the matter ? Furthermore, it was a comfort to have told a considerable portion of the truth to Nell. True, she seemed thoughtful and perturbed at present, but women are odd creatures ; very likely she would be quite herself again before they could reach the house.

"Take my arm, Nellie," he concluded cheerfully, "and let us go up the garden together. I'm anxious to see Jack Syme, and get the business out of hand."

Nell made a strong effort to put aside her doubts entirely, and put but one question to him as they strolled up the steep gravel path. "How does a man make enemies, Terence ?"

"Nothing easier, dear, for a man who's a

doctor. Every patient is a potential enemy. You cure him, and all's well; you fail to do so as quickly as he thinks his due, and he grumbles; you fail altogether, and he hates you. Then he calls in another doctor, and Nature perhaps rights him of her own accord, while the other doctor gets the credit—and your carelessness and stupidity become that patient's nearest and dearest grievance. Then you send in your bill, and the breach is complete."

"Certainly people are more unjust and ungrateful than I imagined."

"Worse in every way than you imagined, little one. Men don't think of justice; but only of getting their money's worth. As for gratitude, why 'tis a pretty thing to read of in books."

Nell sighed, but made no effort to combat these views. But if Terence was thus laying down the law in a superior manner, as becomes a man, she was meanwhile influencing him for good, as becomes a woman. Save for the fear of displeasing her, it is probable that his present good resolution would have gone the way of most of his others, passing gently through procrastination to oblivion. Not that Nell urged him by a single word to go straight to Jack Syme, but he knew she expected this, and he left her the moment they entered the house.

Finding his assistant in the surgery, he opened the question at once, explained that he had lately seen a good deal of Ezekiel, and from one thing and another had been led to suspect the existence of an aortic aneurism.

Jack listened, shrugging his shoulders. He totally disbelieved in any ailment of Ezekiel's other than hysteria.

"The man's a hysterical fool," he exclaimed, as he had done many times before; the truth being that Jack was in some respects a fool himself, though of quite a different order. He had no imagination, and a morbid, sensitive, intense man like poor Doidge was necessarily a closed book to him. Moreover, he had always looked upon Terence as too subtle and fanciful in his diagnoses, though capable often of making phenomenally good shots under difficult circumstances.

Later in the day, however, Syme found the miller in a tolerably favourable mood, and in obedience to orders carried out the desired physical examination with such skill as he possessed.

"Have you seen Doidge?" asked Terence, when his assistant returned.

"Oh yes, I've seen him, and gone through all the usual hocus-pocus; and I believe your aneurism to be a mare's nest."

"Well, after all, perhaps you're right," said Terence.

CHAPTER V.

WHEN the summer and early autumn had passed; when cricket was over and the crops had been gathered in; when the weary British subaltern, exhausted by cricket, tennis, C. O.'s parades, whist, billiards, and other such labours incident to the military career, was beginning to think of rest and peace in the bosom of his family; in a word, towards the end of October, the return of Captain Julius Rush, of the 20th Dragoon Guards, was being eagerly looked for at Bickington Park.

The old squire was to have his son with him for two whole months this time, and was somewhat unhinged by the contemplation of such a prospect. Sleep became a thing of difficulty for him ; and, once the great day was fixed, time appeared to come to a stand-still. His mind began to run upon railway accidents ; the condition of a certain railway bridge about forty miles on the London side of Chillington, about which some doubtful rumours were afloat, became a matter for searching inquiry. But, though some days of nervous agitation had gone far towards making the happy climax seem impossible, the down express did actually land Captain Julius, quite unharmed, upon the Chillington platform at the appointed hour. Whereupon Squire Rush seized upon his son, feeling younger by ten years than he had done an hour before, and enjoyed a most luxurious drive, with the young summertide in his heart contradicting any gloomy impressions made by the fading autumn woods around him.

"Dear lad!" he exclaimed, "I'm no better than an old woman about you. Do you know—— But I really can't confess to such folly."

But, encouraged by the captain's smile, he did confess.

"Do you know that I've been so fidgety about the rumoured rottenness of that bridge, that I had serious thoughts of offering to repair it at my own expense?"

Julius laughed so that the mare shied and swerved.

"It's a fact, dear lad; I did actually contemplate such a thing!"

The squire laughed as heartily as his son, and they went on chattering nonsense for some time like any brace of schoolboys.

"Ah!" said the old man, as they presently drove through the lodge gates, "if you would but take a wife and retire, and come to live with me at Bickington, I should have nothing left to wish for."

"What wife would welcome me home as
you have done, my dear dad ? Why, with
my surly temper I should quarrel finally with
any woman before the honeymoon was half
over. No matrimony for me, thank you ; I
don't want to be under the thumb of any
mortal thing in petticoats. I've seen too
many good fellows mangled by that same
toothed-trap, matrimony, to care about
putting my own foot into it."

"Well, I'm glad Miss Kate can't hear
him," muttered the squire with a sigh.
" He's just as stiff-necked as ever, I fear."

Julius found sweet peace reigning at the
park, and the master of the house a changed
person. Mr. Rush's nerve power was fairly
well restored ; he was capable now of speak-
quite boldly to his servants, that is, in
courageous moments. There was laxity in
the house, no doubt, but the atmosphere of
the place was now kindly and genial ; with
an undercurrent of sympathy between master

and men such as Julius was pleased to note. He had come down fully prepared to make a second earthquake in the establishment, but perceived before he had been an hour in the house that neither speech nor action would be called for this time. The bold surgery of his last visit had wrought a complete cure ; the general tone of Bickington Park was now that of one of Cuyp's pastorals.

Although he hardly knew one flower from another, it was Julius Rush's first duty on the occasion of every home-coming to make a tour of the conservatories with the squire on his arm, listening to such local news as the latter had to pour forth. The rite was duly performed to-day soon after his arrival, and much home-talk safely got through during the process.

There was a good deal of local gossip to be dealt with this time. The old squire rambled from topic to topic with the ardour

of one who catches a sympathetic listener
but once a year and makes the most of him
when caught; but his talk to-day had a
knack of coming round, after a multitude of
side excursions, into one main channel.

In truth, the whole district was now wag-
ging its tongue, not about Simon Secretan,
whose final departure from the country had
seemed a fitting close to his marred career,
but about his more interesting successor;
and Mr. Rush was hardly original enough to
avoid being carried along in so powerful a
stream. This central figure, upon whom all
eyes seemed to be focused, was not that of a
special favourite of Captain Rush's, although
he could not help admitting that the man's
story was curious and picturesque in its way.
Only the other day this popular hero had
been a penniless searcher after a small
medical practice; now he was a master, at
least during his wife's lifetime, of a fine old
hall, and had the spending of an enormous

income.   For to such an elevation had
Terence Clancy risen—the Terence whom
we saw but a few months since on the brink
of a miserable confession to his wife.

The breeze of fortune which landed
Terence upon this pinnacle of prosperity
sent a thrill of excitement, rather than surprise, through the neighbourhood.   Mrs.
French-Chichester had long since given up
her own hopes in favour of Nell and Terence ;
and other shrewd eyes had seen this climax
looming in the distance for some time.   Even
dull ones, judging by the after-asseverations
of their owners, must have had occasional
glimpses of it.   At any rate, there was little
astonishment openly expressed, though a
perfect buzz of romantic interest and speculation arose from Chillington and went eddying
through half the county.

When, towards the end of a wet depressing
hay-harvest, the news of Sir Hamo Secretan's
death got spread abroad, a few days of

delightful curiosity supervened; but the
period of pleasant suspense was brief. The
general drift of the will, made and executed
but a few days before the baronet's death,
soon became known.

Sir Hamo might be said to cease to live,
rather than to die, so placid and serene was
his final departure. And during those last
few peaceful days of his life there did arise
in the old man's breast a certain yearning
after his son Simon, who had disgraced
him, had gone away out of the country, no
one knew whither, had caused him bitter
disappointment and pain; but who in old
days, despite his tiresome whims and fancies,
had certainly loved his father.

Troubled by this vague longing, and
perhaps with some remembrance of neglect
on his own part, Sir Hamo did begin to
speak of his son to Nell and Terence Clancy.
The latter, pricked by remorse—which was
often sharp with him, though seldom long-

lived—now earnestly desired to establish
Simon's innocence in his father's eyes before
it should be too late; but his lips were sealed
by his own previous assertions to Nell. It
was impossible to go back upon those former
statements now; he had proposed to himself
to become gradually converted to Simon's
innocence, but there was no time for such a
process. It was bad to be a liar in his own
eyes, absolutely impossible to be one in hers.
He had to keep lying on to the end, and was
miserable enough under the task.

On the morning of his death Sir Hamo,
for the first time, put the downright question,
"Do you think my son ever did that
thing of which he was publicly accused, or
was it only insane pride that kept him
silent?"

Even now, at the eleventh hour, if only
Nell had been absent, Terence might have
wrought himself up to the point of freeing
Simon from the charge; but Sir Hamo

would scarcely let her out of his sight. The question was put in her presence, and with a pang of bitter self-loathing, Terence told the culminating lie of his life—the lie that had existed in his mind potentially ever since the treacherous thought of putting his own guilt upon Simon was first bred out of the fear of discovery.

He tried to console himself afterwards with the reflection that the admission would have come too late to affect the question of Simon's inheritance ; but the consolation was inadequate, for, for aught he knew to the contrary, Sir Hamo might have altered his will at once ; nor did the final scene take place for some hours afterwards. It was not until late in the afternoon that Sir Hamo, reclining in his invalid chair upon the terrace, sent a last feeble gaze over the beloved woods of Hollacomb, where his heart still lingered, and sank with a quiet sigh into his last sleep.

Very soon the discovery that his wife had

inherited the bulk of Sir Hamo's property, and was actually standing in Simon's shoes, came upon Terence with a shock that half stunned him. At first he was only stupefied with astonishment, then remorseful and ecstatically happy by turns. He had never imagined that Sir Hamo would thus put his son entirely aside, and his remorse at the unlooked-for catastrophe was poignant. On the other hand, he had never imagined that he should one day, without a single conscious effort to that end, find himself the wielder of a vast income.

But the wondrous intoxication of possession soon ousted all other feelings. He was almost beside himself; ceased for a time to believe in his own identity. The glamour of wealth and power worked in his veins like an elixir. In old days his highest flights of fancy had never touched the mountain peak upon which he now actually stood. He seemed to have been transported to paradise, while the clang of the gates behind him rang the knell of all past trouble and pain and harassment.

As he grew cooler, sophistical arguments came thick and fast at his bidding; a brief for his defence was built up with a facility surprising even to himself. He had never stirred a finger to bring about Simon's disinheritance, had never conceived the thing possible. Simon had done it himself. Years of proud aloofness, of obstinate silence when soft speech was needed, of frequent irritation of his father's prejudices, had made this result inevitable. The public indictment of Simon was but an incident in the long quarrel of a lifetime. Nor was Simon left destitute, or even poor, in his exile; his property of Hollacomb would always bring him in a good income. Again, if it were possible, he, Terence, would be relieved to let Nell hand over to Simon a handsome proportion of what he might have looked upon as his due;

but it soon became apparent that nothing of the sort could be done. It was found that Nell could not touch the bulk of the property during her lifetime ; and should she desire to ease her mind by devising it to Simon at her death, Terence would never dream of dissuading her.

With these and countless other arguments did Terence crowd the imaginary foolscap of his brief; then, having demolished in the process every possible counterclaim that his conscience might elaborate, he mentally revised the whole and put it aside for the present, while he plunged anew into the surge of happiness which Fate had rolled to his feet.

Upon this topic of the new prince of Monks Damerel, his social successes, his lavish generosity, his phenomenal popularity, Squire Rush was still expatiating when he and Julius sat down to luncheon. Indeed, the dragoon had already heard so much

about the hero of the hour that, " not to die
a listener," he compromised the question by
agreeing to drive his father over to Chillington in the course of the afternoon, and hear
Terence Clancy speak for himself.   For the
affairs of the cricket season were to be wound
up at a general meeting of the club at three
o'clock, when its new captain-president,
Squire Clancy, as the principal speaker and
great star of the occasion, could be studied
in all his new glory.

Satisfied with this compromise, Mr. Rush
was soon inditing of a more interesting
matter—that is, his improved relations with
Miss Tredethlyn.   The friendly feeling
between her and himself had maintained
itself during the summer; had even increased a little, though of his ancient fear
there still lingered enough to make the
road to Moor Gates a somewhat steep one.
In fact, it usually took the old squire, though
he made no confession to that effect, from ten

days to a fortnight to screw himself up to
the point of achieving a call upon the Tredethlyns. It appeared that he owed Mr.
Tredethlyn a call now, and, with his son's
support, would like to pay it soon. Would
Julius come with him in a day or two?

An absence of some months, however,
had not softened the stubborn Julius. He
listened calmly, asked no questions, committed himself to nothing, whereat the
squire's disappointment was sufficiently
patent. His long-cherished desire to have
his grandchildren playing about his knee
seemed as far as ever from fulfilment; for he
was well assured that Julius, if he did not
marry Kate, would inevitably die a bachelor.
Yet Mr. Rush had not by any means fired
his last shot. Under pressure of failure this
simple old man was growing cunning.

"You've heard nothing of Captain Saunderson and his wife, I suppose?" he presently
asked, in a casual voice.

"No—nothing at all."

"I verily believe," the squire continued, with an innocent-sounding laugh, "that were the humbly born aunt living in our neighbourhood, the homelier presence would solace your pride even to the point of making you civil to Miss Kate. Mrs. Saunderson's 'commonness' and 'vulgarity,' which I heard so much about at the vicarage that afternoon, would be a constant balm to your mightiness. Wouldn't they, now?"

Julius was taken aback by this shrewd probing of his weakness. He said nothing —would not permit himself to smile—but there was a gleam in his eye that the simple cunning father noted and treasured up. And so acute a schemer was his son's frowardness making of the old gentleman, that he said not a word more at present, but changed the subject with a certain triumphant subtlety.

When, at the hour appointed for the

cricket meeting, they drew up before the entrance of the old town hall, Julius was able to realize by ocular evidence what a good deal of talk had put before him in but a hazy fashion—to wit, the remarkable pitch of popularity to which Terence Clancy had attained.

Under the arches of the hall and about the gravel space which lay between the ancient building and the road a large crowd was gathered ; and when a smart tandem-cart came flashing over the town bridge, there arose a murmur that presently swelled into a downright cheer. The young prince received an ovation and evidently revelled in it.

In truth, popularity was as the breath of life to Terence Clancy. He possessed the natural kindliness which seeks public appro-val, and was free from the arrogance that withers it. Moreover, his character, at least in regard to the qualities which make for heart-winning, was of a kind to bloom and expand under the sun of prosperity. His simple vanity took no harm from a little kindly applause. As they cheered him now his delicate skin flushed like a rose, his eyes sparkled with pleasure, his smile was bright and happy as summer waves sun-smitten. Old men upon whom that smile fell thought of their boyhood; young men who caught it hoped their sweethearts might be looking another way.

" There, now—did I exaggerate ? " cried Mr. Rush, triumphantly. " You see for yourself how he takes hold of people and charms them. Isn't he a brilliant, handsome, dashing young fellow, now ? "

But Julius vouchsafed his father nothing but a sardonic murmur. It vexed him to find this usurper of Simon's throne wielding the sceptre with such triumphant success. How much did the man really care for the public which revered him in this fulsome

way ?   When had Simon, who for years had
lavished heart and money upon this people,
ever been cheered in the public street ?
Who missed him now, or cared whether he
were alive or dead ?   In short, the soldier's
naturally gloomy view of human nature was
heightened by this incident ; and, as a man
who had always succeeded better in winning
respect than love, he was perhaps somewhat
jealous on his own account as well as
Simon's.   He certainly entered the hall and
took a seat beside his father with a growing
resentment against the general enthusiasm
of the gathering.

Some one in the gallery watched Captain
Rush's passage across the room, and, noting
the dark mood of his countenance, felt depressed and disappointed.   She was conscious of being perfectly dressed and of
looking really handsome ; for Mrs. French-
Chichester—whose old friendship for Terence
had lately returned in full force, and who

never let slip a chance of being agreeable to Nell and Kate nowadays—had paid her one or two charming compliments. But of what avail to be admittedly worth looking at when people won't throw a glance your way, or give you a chance of bowing to them ?

However, Kate had a sharp pair of eyes at her side, and could not afford to parade her mortification. She would not even permit herself the solace of cynical remarks in general, but talked so charitably of various people in the throng below that Mrs. French-Chichester secretly voted her a bore, and suppressed her yawns with difficulty.

Mr. Tredethlyn, as chairman of the meeting, presently opened the proceedings with his old, pleasant, genial commonplaces, while Kate, listening to her father with an enthusiasm somewhat abated by habit, was irresistibly reminded of that stormy first assembly of the club, when Simon was so bitterly outraged. From which it appears that Julius Rush was not the only person whose thoughts wandered away regretfully to the exile.

After the chairman's opening speech, two or three of the most determined bores in the place addressed the hall in succession, depressing the spirits of the assembly with much success. Indeed, five-and-twenty minutes of such eloquence seemed to charge the very atmosphere of the room with droning stock phrases, such as "continued prosperity," "creditable exhibition of cricketing talent," and the like.

Mrs. French-Chichester, after muttering, "I didn't know this was to be a prayer-meeting," fell into a gentle doze at this stage of the proceedings, leaving Kate free at least to direct her eyes whither she pleased.

When the sufferings of the assembly, however, had reached to about the furthest limit of human endurance, the last of those honest citizens, whose vanity so unfortunately

flew to the tongue, showed signs of exhaus-
tion, and proceeded to wind up his speech
by a eulogium upon the most active, most
popular, most enterprising member of the
club—to wit, its captain-president, Mr.
Terence Clancy of Monks Damerel Hall.

Whereupon the audience awoke suddenly,
as though under a sprinkle of fresh water,
and a cheery rapping of sticks began. The
eulogy took a little time to get bodied forth,
and contained long words enough to make
a plain man dizzy ; but at length they flailed
it to death with gladsome " Hear hears !" and
so won the breathing space long craved.

They were in a mood now for something
bright and jestful—and they got it.

Terence was in splendid trim ; and so
bubbled with wit and drollery, that the
room was soon full of volleying laughter,
which renewed itself almost with his every
sentence.

Out of the considerable throng of profiles

that came within Kate's field of vision, all save one were twitching and wrinkling with spasms of mirth ; that one looked indifferent, if not critical, and presently took an expression even less in key with the general feeling of the audience.

The speaker had been describing with much point and sly humour how the great bowler, Dick Yelverton, had missed an easy catch, and in doing so had received the cricket-ball full in his right eye, towards the end of the last match of the season ; and he rounded off these remarks with a quotation not a bit too trite for his audience.

" Dick wasn't pretty to look at, if you remember," he said with a sly chuckle, " and, faith, there's a beautiful halo of autumn tints round his eye yet. Look at him, you whose wickets he has scattered so often and so unkindly ! Ah, but Dick's our prince of bowlers still, despite that wicked piece of leather : for what says the poet ?—

' You may break, you may shatter the vase, as you will,
But the scent of the roses will hang round it still.' "

Now, what could there be in this well-worn couplet, Kate asked herself, to impress Captain Rush so curiously?

At first Rush could not tell himself, but the words did startle him unaccountably. It was as though he had heard a sudden shout while walking in a desert place. Kate watched his face grow puzzled, then still more intent, then absent-looking, then completely mystified; lastly, full of vague darkness and suspicion. She knew that Captain Rush had never subscribed to the popular verdict in Terence's favour, had, indeed, always spoken of him with frank dislike; but Terence had spoken brightly and genially enough, without a hint of arrogance or self-importance. Surely there was not a word in his harangue even for an enemy to grow sullen about!

The captain's speech concluded the proceedings, and the crowd proceeded to jostle itself, in excellent spirits, down the steps and out on to the gravel; Terence himself driving off, flushed and radiant, with cheers and good wishes still ringing in his ears.

Upon descending from the gallery, Kate was greeted by the man whose profile she had been studying with so much artistic interest, but who had not thrown a single glance her way during the proceedings. His manner was distant and formal, his words few; but he did speak, and did hand her into her pony-carriage. Perhaps he found it necessary to give himself this little treat as a reward for previous resolute conduct.

Yet, though his speech was calm enough, Kate thought Captain Rush must be putting some constraint upon himself. He looked uneasy and excited, and—though she made the admission to herself with some mortification—somewhat absent-minded.

She gathered up her reins and made a

show of starting, but he still remained in a conversational attitude ; though, his stock of conventional remarks being apparently exhausted, he might have been expected to say good-bye with alacrity.

"I shall make the baldest remark I can possibly think of, then he'll be glad to get rid of me," muttered Kate. "What did you think of the speeches this afternoon, Captain Rush ?"

"Oh, capital. Yes, the air is pleasantly cool, and you'll have a pleasant drive home. I beg your pardon," he added apologetically, "but I didn't quite catch your question. Would you mind driving on a few yards out of the way of the people ? I want to speak to you about the detective and his verdict."

"Pray tell me all about it," said Kate, anxiously, as soon as they had passed out of hearing of the crowd. Captain Rush was walking beside the pony-carriage, his face still wearing the look of puzzled disquiet which she had noticed some time since.

" Well, to tell the plain truth "—he smiled slightly as he made this confession—" the man was a complete failure."

"Ah! you should have taken my advice, and gone at once to Mr. Doidge."

" That is preceisely what I did."

" Yes, yes. Had he no clue to give you ? "

" The poor crazy fellow knows no more than we do, and will never make any discovery worth thinking about. He agreed to work away during my absence, but I don't for a moment suppose that he'll ever penetrate the mystery."

"Are you equally hopeless of success yourself ? I do hope you won't give the thing up in despair ? "

" I never give things up," he said curtly.

" I'm glad to think there'll be one friend still working for poor old Simon. Are you still groping quite blindly ? Is there no ray of light from any direction ? "

" Nothing worth calling a ray, perhaps,"— he paused some moments before giving this reply—" yet within the last twenty-four hours a kind of glimmer has come. I can't tell you more than that, and perhaps I'm mistaken in calling it even a glimmer. Suspicion is a reckless leaper, and mere personal prejudice may give it a fillip in any direction. Moreover, even supposing—what at present I have no right whatever to suppose—but the fact is, I'm in a state of bewilderment to-night, and maundering on in a way which can only puzzle and vex you —and the best thing I can do will be to say good night at once."

Certainly Kate was not a little bewildered by his words and manner, while at the same time comforted at finding him willing to offer her such a modicum of attention as he had permitted himself. When she drove off into the darkness, it was with a tingling consciousness that their hands had met for a moment, and that even a fraction of a second may contain something worth carrying away—and perhaps thinking about all the way home.

CHAPTER VI.

"HOW'D ye like to see me a Member
of Parliament, Nellie mavourneen?"

Nell smiled at her husband somewhat
doubtfully, having learned to associate a
relapse into his native brogue with some
attempt or other to wheedle away her better
judgment.

"I think you'd be a chameleon of a politician, Terence; a Liberal one day——"

"Deuce a bit of it, Nell!" he cut in with
a deep twinkle in his eye, "for, odds weather-
cocks! (as Bob Acres might say) I'll be a
hot Tory before this week's out, and keep so
for the remainder of me natural life. I've

contracted Toryism like a virulent disease ;
and, faith, I can't afford to take any curative
medicine ! "

" Why, only yesterday you told me you
were a Liberal, Terence ? "

" An' so I was, me dear, until nine p.m.,
or thereabouts ; but the Tory poison worked
its way into me system after dinner last night.
Bridistow and Pigott inoculated me, with
Mrs. French-Chichester to help 'um ; and
I'm not likely to take a turn for the better
this side of the Millennium—unless they
happen to treat me to cold shoulder. I'll
explain further, little girl, so keep your pretty
ears open. Up till a month ago, I was a
Fenian, because, being free from any taint
of political ambition, I could afford to think
straight ; then a woman tempted me—that
is to say, Mrs. French-Chichester conceived
for me the notion of a parliamentary career
—and I fell away into Liberalism. Now,
however, it seems that the Tory system of

humbug is likely to land me in the House of
Commons more readily than the other, so a
Tory I am already, of the grand old full-
bodied fruity sort; none stauncher to be
found in all broad England, none truer to
our grand old institutions, our Church, our
Sovereign, our caste prejudice, our innate
stupidity, and the other time-honoured and
colossal things that go to make us English
gentlemen what we are! Such noble
sentiments have I imbibed, little Nell, in the
course of but a few hours; or, to put it
another way, such is the first hand dealt me,
and which I'm bound to play, do you see?"

"Not in the least at present."

"Well, then, I'll compress the whole
question into a nutshell for you. The Liberal
member for this division of the county is an
old crock, who will not stand again at the
next General Election; thus, when a certain
penniless Irish adventurer became the other
day a person of importance, the Liberals of

this neighbourhood began to view him as a possible successor to the ancient crock aforesaid. They made wary but definite advances to the adventurer-personage, and found him both intelligent and sympathetic, insomuch that he promised to develop into a thorough-going people's man in due time. So far, so good ; but now for the cross-current which has drawn this open-hearted young fellow into another channel.

"Our Tory member is young, but a brain-less fool—you see I take this last opportunity of speaking quite candidly before undertaking the yoke of a professional politician ; do not fear that blunt and hardy truthfulness will ever distinguish (and condemn) me hereafter —I say frankly, he's a brainless fool, and my countrymen in the House (more power to 'um !) smother him with ridicule before ever the foolish tongue can wag off a brace of sentences. Wherefore his good friends down here are sick of the long-eared representative, and live in hopes of getting him to resign long before the next General Election. Now do you see how the land lies? The Irish adventurer has been playing off one party against the other, but will one day this week, in all probability, commit himself to the greater dullards, as being the more efficient props. As he only lives on his wife's charity, his exalted position needs an artificial buttress here and there, dy'e see? He can't afford to do without the wealthy big-wig, Sir Raby Pigott, his serene and intellectual high-ness, Lord Bridistow, and the other landed geniuses of the district. In fact, my dear Nell, the long and short of it is, that, to-morrow being market-day, I am to meet Bridistow in the town about noon for further political discussion, and shall probably bring him here to lunch; finally yielding to his blandishments, after due modest assertion of my own unworthiness, about four o'clock in the afternoon."

" But, Terence, surely common honesty—"

" I don't care the flick of a whip for that, bless your simplicity. I tell you I'm going to be a leading man, to have my fling among these English fools—whom at bottom I hate with all my soul ! I started life as a pauper, sprung from a long line of paupers ground down by English tyranny, and now, by the Lord, I'll have my fling ! I've purchased popularity by a little blarney—bedad, you should have heard the fools cheer me at the cricket meeting yesterday !—and now am going to purchase a high place by adding thereto your money, so ye'd best make up your mind to the situation, little woman."

It will be seen that prosperity had exhilarated Terence, and emphasized some of his qualities in a peculiar fashion. This audacious method of handling his wife was the one he commonly used now, for he found that by persistent self-confidence and assertion he could bluff her into almost anything. In truth, Terence had learned the secret of how to get his own way from no less able an instructress than Mrs. French-Chichester, who had been of great service to the young master of Monks Damerel lately, and had taken up the question of his parliamentary career with great enthusiasm ; indeed, but for her, Terence might never have turned his thoughts to public life. She was ambitious for him, determined to make him a leading man in the county, and full of a hundred schemes for pushing him up to the highest rungs of the social ladder. Nor would she have asked a pleasanter task than the training and handling of so promising a candidate for popular favour. She it was who taught him the value of social trifles, the importance of ingratiating himself not only with the best people, but with all persons, high and low ; who fed him full with the strong meat of worldly ambition, and saw that his moral consciousness should not be unduly worked upon by his wife. In truth, but for her support and wise counsel, it is probable that Nell would hardly have been brought so soon into her present condition of wholesome submission ; for the sprightly widow had from the first laid herself out to preserve Terence from the ignominy of being henpecked. She would carry him off triumphantly from under Nell's very nose, and persuade him that his wife was flatly unsympathetic, undutifully cold in all matters relating to the only question worth thinking about—his future high career. She sneered Nell down as good-humouredly and as effectually as she had formerly done her cousin Simon ; for if this active woman was romantically prone to bring likely young people together, she was not less skilled at gently drawing them asunder afterwards.

Having delivered himself of the above frank statement of his political views and intentions, Terence turned, whistling cheerfully, to look at a modern sea-piece placed upon an easel near which Nell was seated. She watched him furtively as he followed the lines of the composition with his finger and criticised, with muttered exclamations of satisfaction, the delicate opal tints of the sky horizon.

The general appearance of the room, lately Sir Hamo Secretan's study, suggested that the new master of the hall had already made a pretty fair beginning of the joyous pastime which he called "having his fling." The chamber was now a perfect gallery of modern French and English pictures, evidently chosen by one who had no taste for mediocrity; the new furniture was the richest obtainable; the table was covered with costly nick-nacks, while a goodly pile of unopened tradesmen's bills, the crop of a single post-delivery, occupied one corner. In truth, the quiet old hall seemed not merely to have awakened from a long sleep, but to have

been hailed upon by a goodly shower of
gold. A bevy of smart London servants
had replaced the innocent dovecote of Mrs.
Henley, who had retired to a fashionable
watering-place with a view to setting up as
a gentlewoman at large. Terence already
possessed an excellent stud, and a little army
of grooms and helpers ; also a hundred-ton
cutter at Lymport, and many other appur-
tenances necessary to a man of his wealth.
It was not his policy to hide his light under
a bushel, but rather to let it flare, bonfire-
fashion, across the breadth of the county.
Nor was he troubled with any paltry misgivings as to expense. Whenever his agent
—the very man who had first caused the tin-
mine to shed pure gold into Sir Hamo's
pockets — waited upon the new squire,
Terence would exclaim, with his genial
laugh—

"Oh, d—n the business, Treluddra—go
to Mrs. Clancy about everything ; the pro-

perty's hers, and faith, she must take the bother with it!"

"Do you see the curl of foam on this breaking wave, Nell?" he now said after a pause. "It is done with one stroke of the palette-knife, but a life-time of labour and study have gone to make that one stroke possible. Now the real art of life is to clutch the success without the labour. I'm going to do just such a perfect stroke to-morrow, and the only toil that has gone to produce it has been that of winning the sweetest wife in England. Ah, 'tis her presence that has kept all but landscapes and sea-scapes from these walls, for no painted head's worth looking at beside the 'ripe and real' beauty that I have always before me!"

Nell accepted this sweetmeat with a dutiful smile, suppressing the sigh that would have come more glibly. She was glad that he had rattled on without giving her much chance of replying, for her old influence over Terence had dwindled to the point where judicious silence has to take the place of conscientious objection.

We know how, on the last occasion of our seeing them together, she had resolutely set herself to accept her husband as he was ; to love and, if possible, respect him, limitations and all. To that course of conduct she had clung with stubborn fidelity, and none would ever know how much it cost her. The trial had begun at once, for the most earnest endeavour to accept his explanation had proved futile. It was plain to her, as soon as coolness returned, that he had some dark secret on his mind, that he had glided from the very brink of confession by one of those slippery turns which seemed to come to him so easily. Well, she would never pry into that, never allude to it again ; and certainly the trouble, whatever it might be, had been driven clean out of his mind when the rise

of fortune came, unless his constant desire
for fresh excitement might be interpreted
as—— But no; Nell would have nothing
to do with interpretations and surmises. Perhaps she felt that the less she knew the
better her chance of happiness.

Howbeit, from that time Terence had
begun as it were to slip from her grasp. He
openly resented her scruples as to stepping
into Simon's shoes, and could never endure
even to have Simon's name mentioned. He
plunged into all social dissipations that lay
open to him with a kind of feverish energy,
and threw money about in a lavish way which
frightened his quiet-going wife ; nor did he
seem to care much about pleasing her or
retaining her respect, sustained as he now
was by the intoxicating applause of a large
neighbourhood. But still Nell persisted in
making every allowance for him, in manu-
facturing excuses for every fresh whim and
vagary of her husband. In truth, she was like

a friendly woman-critic standing before the canvas of one who is dear to her, striving to find here and there a brush-mark of genius in a broad spread of flat mediocrity.

"Well, good-bye, little woman," said Terence at length, when his wife had re- mained silent for some minutes; "apparently I'm not destined to elicit any sympathy from you, so I may as well be off. You can't enter into a man's ambition at all, I suppose. Sorry I can't fall in with your views either, which I presume would tend to the parcelling out of the property into cabbage-gardens for the poor, or building-sites for almshouses. Sorry I can't ride a beastly tricycle instead of a thoroughbred horse, or drive you to market of a Thursday in a donkey-cart. Sorry I'm not a goody-goody country curate, with a taste for distributing flannels and fawning on old women. However, I've a notion that 'twould be all the same. Were I the Angel Gabriel, you'd be only half satisfied with me ; certainly nothing composed of mere flesh and blood can ever pretend to come up to your standard."

"You insult me—you insult me !" cried Nell, with quivering lips.

It was the first time Nell had ever " flown out " at him, as the homely phrase has it ; and the man's natural kindliness was at once awakened.

" There, there, little girl. I know my tone was abominable, and my words nearly as bad. Forgive me, Nellie !"

"Oh, Terence, I never shall be happy in this miserable place. I feel that it doesn't rightly belong to me, that we are flinging away money which is not our own. Our position seems to me altogether false and hollow, and honesty seems to have become an impossibility. Why must we always be scheming to better ourselves, and straining after fresh social successes ? Why must you go against your conscience and pretend to

hold political views which you really hate ?
How much happiness do we get from all
this false striving ? I wish—ah, how I wish !
—we were back in our old life, honestly
trying to make both ends meet, and to save
a little, and caring for nothing beyond ! "

" What mawkish nonsense ! " cried Terence
impatiently. " Was ever a man so worried
and bothered just for trying to do his best
and get on in the world ? I let you take
your own course, and mope at home when
you ought to be furthering my chances in
society. I never harass you or put the least
pressure on you—and yet you're never con-
tented for an hour."

" Because I don't feel *honest*, Terence ;
and the more I think of our position the less
satisfied I feel about it. I can't see that we
have any right to be standing in Simon's
shoes—— "

" Look here, Nell," he interposed angrily ;
" I wish you'd understand once for all that I

will not hear a word more about that man.
You drive me half crazy with continual
harping on that string. You've taught me
to hate the man so that I wish he were
dead! How could I prevent his disinheritance? How could I reconcile him with
his father, when they had been pulling two
ways all their lives? I have enough to bear
in the knowledge that you respect and revere
the man as you've never respected me, without having the loss of his property thrust in
my face like this!"

"Yes, I do respect him," said Nell, firmly;
"for it has come to me—I know not how—
that he was never guilty of that wickedness.
It was not in Simon's nature to do such a
thing, and I ought never to have believed
in his guilt."

"What do you mean?" cried Terence,
who was now white with anger.

"Just what I say—that Simon had nothing
to do with poor Mary's trouble."

"What are you driving at? Whom do you suspect?"

"Why are you so fierce and strange, Terence? I suspect no one, I only long for the real culprit to be found and the innocent man righted. Ah, if I only had it in my power to punish the man who has ruined poor Simon——"

"You wouldn't spare him, I suppose?"

"After what he has done for Simon, I should be merciless towards him!"

"God help him, if you do catch him! He had better have drowned himself at once than have injured your hero!"

"Well, well," said Nell, with a heavy sigh, "I ought not to have introduced a subject that pains you so much, Terence. I know I have done wrong, but you shan't be troubled about this any more. Tell me further about your political views, for I am sure you were joking with me in pretending to be so hypocritical?"

"I've neither views, nor hope, nor ambition," he muttered. "I'm a poor, miserable devil, always straining after happiness and never reaching it! I wish, with you, that we had never left our old life — or rather that we had gone abroad, and started a new one, and left this cursed country for ever!"

Accustomed though she was to Terence's sudden changes of mood, Nell was amazed at this one. He had plunged from hot wrath into flat depression with a speed which almost took her breath away.

"I have vexed and worried you, dear," she said penitently. "And I do believe my views are very narrow and peculiar. Nor have I any right to expect you to think with me in everything. Let us talk of something happy and pleasant now, such as our plans for next summer. Are you really going to take me for that yachting cruise to Scotland?"

But Terence's fit of despondency was not to be shaken off so easily.

"Life's a poor thing, Nell," he groaned, "brimful of shams and frauds and irony. And our insane pursuit of happiness is the most pitiful thing under the sun. Can you name a single living soul who is happy ?

> ' Happy thou art not :
> For what thou hast not still thou striv'st to get,
> And what thou hast forgett'st.'

Do you know that speech of the duke's in *Measure for Measure?* I know every line of it, and every line's as true as it is pathetic.

> ' If thou art rich, thou art poor ;
> For, like an ass whose back with ingots bows,
> Thou bear'st thy heavy riches but a journey,
> And death unloads thee.   Friend hast thou none.'

Most true, Nell—most true! Friend I have none. They call me the most popular man in the county; but there's not a living soul that cares for me but you—and even you

would fall off if you knew me through and
through. I wonder, could any man afford
to be known through and through? If
there be such a man, I'll admit that he's
happy. I'd rather be like such a one than
be a crowned king, though maybe the possession of an absolutely clear conscience would
be a happiness insupportable by a poor devil
like me! Man's nothing but a doomed
creature, struggling over ground honey-
combed with pitfalls, into one or other of
which he *must* fall sooner or later; then
the devil throws a net over him, and he
never fronts the clear sky more. Look, Nell
—look where I'm pointing! Do you see how
the sunlight falls on that field by the edge
of the wood yonder? and do you see that
stooping figure on the grass? That's the
figure of a man, and he's snaring larks. He
has a net set upright and the cord in his
hand, and grain spread close to the net.
Watch him now! See, he jerks the cord,

and the net falls, and the hulking brute darts forward, doubtless to clutch the little fluttering victim. Next he'll put it into a cage, six inches by four, to yearn away its life henceforth in some dismal alley. It will never more feel the glorious sweep of the spring breeze, nor the warm kiss of the June sunshine, but just long and pine and yearn away its heart till it breaks. Now, a man, once entrapped in one of those pitfalls I mentioned, is no better than a caged lark, with no more hope of liberty, no more chance of escape. Do ye think I exaggerate? Ah, Nellie mavourneen, ye don't know what a hell of suffering comes with a sick conscience! Listen, now! I'd like to slash off three years of me life with a single knife-stroke; then I'd like to meet ye again, a free girl, who had never looked twice at another man, to woo and wed ye fair and straight, and carry ye off to some lonely home in the depths of some far-off country, where are no pitfalls for erring men, and there let ye train me up, and dower me with some of your own goodness, and teach me how to live with a conscience pure and crystal clear as your own! Ah, Nell, Nell, if I could only start fair again—start fair and straight from the beginning, with you to help me—I might win something better than the sham happiness that's me lot now!"

He ended with a sob and a broken exclamation, and Nell could only weep with him and pray for him and try in vain to comfort him.

CHAPTER VII.

THE puzzled frame of mind into which the meeting at the town hall had thrown Captain Rush remained with him throughout the night; and next morning, about the hour when the scene described in the last chapter was enacting, he found himself walking into Chillington, still engaged in argument, analysis, speculation, and such-like mental exercises. He was naturally a man of action rather than of thought; but now, for once in a way, had arrived at the point of being unable to decide upon what course to take at a given juncture.

How to verify, or else to clear his mind of, a vague suspicion which at present seemed merely to be floating in his senses, and unable to find a definite anchorage; which, in fact, was rather a quickening of speculation in a given direction than a formulated suspicion. That was the main condition of the problem still demanding a solution. At present he had but a gossamer-thread of evidence to go upon; and, as a fair-minded man, conscious of a strong bias against the suspected person, he feared to be precipitate. On the other hand, he could not be easy in his mind without making some effort towards obtaining the needed verification.

Julius Rush was long upon the road this morning; yet, by the time he reached the town, his spell of solitary thinking did not appear to have had the desired issue. He strolled on to the town bridge with the aspect of a man who had still failed to make up his mind upon some knotty question. After a brief halt on the bridge, however, he bent his steps up-stream, muttering—"Yes, I'll see Doidge again; there'll be no harm done if I'm reasonably cautious."

He went by the road that Terence had followed with so much fear and hesitation on a former occasion; and upon reaching the mill yard was struck, as Terence had been, with its busy and prosperous aspect. But Rush made no pause for a gossip with the foreman; he promptly strode up to the door, looking neither to right nor left, and knocked vigorously.

When Julius was shown into the parlour, the appearance of poor Doidge, the owner of this flourishing business, was certainly not calculated to cheer a man endowed with some of the melancholy of his period. The miller lay upon a sofa, looking worn and haggard, and altogether changed for the worse since Julius Rush's last visit. The glance which used to wander so proudly from this window over the broad meadows had lost its fire and arrogance. When he spoke his greetings, the voice that had laid down the law to all Chillington, had made clerks, and foremen, and tenants tremble in their shoes, was now languid and toneless; but perhaps the most pathetic thing of all about the man was his meekness.

His visitor was really shocked at finding Ezekiel's natural self-importance thus watered down by sickness, and the more so when he noted the hollow cheek and other physical symptoms of decay. But, as a member of the superior sex, Captain Rush's sympathies were, as a matter of course, kept under good control. He quickly proceeded to business.

"Any news, Mr. Doidge? You agreed to work away in my absence, but I fear bad health must have tied you down a good deal."

Doidge smiled strangely.

" Not altogether, mister."

" What! have you chanced upon any clue ? "

" Not exactly *chanced* neither. Happen I've laboured and delved my way to somethin' o' the sort."

" What is it ? Out with your clue if you have one ! "

" Don't you be startin' off that way, captain, or you'll be smashin' a shaft presently. Hows'ever, I'll tell you this much—that I shall yet lay my hands on *he* before I'm carried out of this mill feet first. But now, let us have your news, for your eye tells me you've got some."

" No, I've nothing much to say ; in fact, my suspicions, such as they are, seem too vague to be worth mentioning at present."

Doidge's wan smile broke out again.

" Still afeard of my violence ? " he muttered.

"No, for I'm perfectly capable of restraining that. What I *do* fear is the possible wronging of an innocent man, because I happen to dislike him heartily, and the giving of deep pain and mortification to several other people besides——"

"To some of your own friends, in fact?" asked the other, with a sudden penetrating glance.

"I never said so!" retorted Julius, angrily; "and I'll trouble you not to jump at unauthorized conclusions. Surely you must understand that I don't care to raise a confounded scandal with nothing but a piece of random guesswork to hinge it upon?"

"I understand, sir," said the miller, drily, adding under his breath, "Mayhap I understand rather more than you'm aware of, mister."

"May I have another look at that volume of poems from among your relics, Doidge?"

"Surely you may, sir. Maybe you'll lift

the box—'tis yonder, in the lower drawer o' the cupboard—for yourself?"

Julius did so, and opened the box with a key which the miller now handed to him. Doidge watched him amusedly, rather than intently, as he rapidly turned the leaves from one marked passage to another.

"Ah!" The searcher's voice, when it presently broke the silence, was edged with the triumph he could not quite suppress.

" You may break, you may shatter the vase, as you will,
   But the scent of the roses will hang round it still."

Julius read the couplet aloud, adding hastily, " I have an idea, Doidge!—I'm bound to say I have an idea—but that's all at present. There's not evidence enough to hang a dog upon yet."

"Just so, captain—just so. And how are you goin' to work up your evidence?"

"I don't know; but in any case we must proceed very cautiously. If my leap in the dark should happen to be in the right direction, however, I can at least guess at a reason for Secretan's extraordinary silence."

"Can you really now? Well, that's very clever! But lookee, sir, I won't play with you any longer. I respect your caution and your scruples and all that; but the truth is, there's no need for 'em—as you shall hear presently. You've got your eye on the probable culprit, it seems—or, at any rate, some one who's worth takin' partic'lar notice of. Well, I happen to know a party who can tell us at a glance whether 'tis our man or not. You won't tell me his name, I suppose?"

"I don't think it would be right at this stage of the proceedings."

"Then I'll humour you, sir. But, anyway, you can tell me whether he's high up or low down in the world?"

"He is in a good position."

"Just so; and consequently has a good way to fall."

"Don't make too sure of him, Doidge. Consider what irremediable mischief has come of your over-hasty suspicion in a former case."

"Don't you be alarmed, captain; and hearken now to my record of work during your absence. I've been takin' this ring o' Mary's up and down the line all through the summer; I've shown it to every jeweller in every town within fifty mile o' Chillington. I had been at the job best part o' three months, and was gettin' hopeless-like, when early this week I made one more cast down among the little shops in the heart o' the low-lying part of Lymport; and in a small street, where they mostly sell stinkin' fish and secondhand seamen's outfits, and which I had passed over before as not worth a visit, I found the man as sold this pearl ring to a gentleman just about the date when it must have been given to Mary."

"Is he certain about the ring? Could he swear to it?"

"It has got his own marks on it. He could swear to't anywhere or anywhen."

"Does he remember the gentleman well? Did he take any special note of his appearance? Does he know his name?"

The self-contained soldier was now on fire with excitement. Doidge talked on with the assurance of a man with whom suspense is practically over.

"No; he knows nothing of the gentleman's name, but can swear to his appearance —noticed one or two points which he remembers perfectly."

"What are the points, man? You madden me with your slowness!"

"I'm not goin' to tell you; I may have reasons for caution as well as you. I'm not goin' to let my enemy slip by marching off on a false trail as I did once before. Tell me when and where to find him, and I'll manage to let my identifyin' witness clap eyes to him, and then we shall know where

we are. He's a little beast of a Jew-shop-
man, my witness is, who, I reckon, would
swear to anythin' for gain ; but if he's thrown
across the path of our gentleman accidental
like, I shall know well enough whether the
recognition be a true article or a make-up."

" We'll arrange a day as soon as possible ;
and if the recognition does come off, will you
send word to me at Bickington at once ? "

"Yes, I'll send on the man himself, and
you'll know him fast enough—a little dirty,
hook-nosed villain, five-foot nothing high,
with a grey beard hanging down to's waist."

"Very well, I shall give orders that any
one answering to that description be sent in
to me at once. What do you think of a
market-day for our experiment ? Every one
in the neighbourhood will be driving into
the town at one time or another on that
day."

"Very good ; to-morrow is market-day,
and the sooner the trial comes off the better.

I'll have my little Jew dawdlin' about the High Street and market-place all day to-morrow, from ten o'clock onwards, and I'll be at his side all the while."

"And you might spend some of the time on the town bridge, for almost everybody who lives on the south side of the river will be driving over it in the course of the morning."

"You'm right, sir; and, what's more, one can lounge on the bridge all day without attractin' notice, with half the town for company. Are you goin' now, sir? Well, good-bye; and don't be afeard us'll get the wrong man this time. I reckon us'll either miss fire altogether—or kill!"

CHAPTER VIII.

TERENCE CLANCY'S spasm of remorse passed over for the time, as
many others had done before now, and by
Thursday morning he was once again his
cheery, jubilant self. It was then his turn
to console Nell, who had been a good deal
unhinged by his fit of despair, and who had
not his happy faculty of throwing off a wave
of depression by a mere outpouring of the
heart to a sympathetic listener.

His political aspirations, too, were now
once more in full working order, for Mrs.
French-Chichester had dined at the hall last
night, and re-invested its master with some

of her own ardour and spirit. Our Lady Bountiful, as it happened, always took especial pleasure in these quiet evenings at Monks Damerel; for Nell's ill-concealed jealousy of her influence over Terence was an unfailing source of enjoyment on the one hand; and on the other, the training and development of so apt a pupil as Nell's husband could not fail to be a relishing task.

On this occasion she took more than usual pains to impress upon Terence what a vista of fine possibilities was opening before him, and at the same time gave him precise instructions as to his attitude towards Lord Bridistow on the morrow. Nor was Nell left out in the cold in this matter of advice and encouragement. Mrs. French-Chichester decided that both Sir Raby Pigott and Lord Bridistow, should be brought in to luncheon to-morrow, and gave their intended hostess many useful hints as to the proper reception of these powerful political backers of the future member.

Nell listened passively, and promised to do her best ; but the visitor easily managed to give emphasis to her lukewarmness, and further impress Terence with a sense that his interests would always be neglected by this unsympathetic wife of his.

Next morning things fell out very much as this shrewd prophetess had foretold. Lord Bridistow and Sir Raby met Terence at the Falcon according to appointment, and in due course were brought on to Monks Damerel. They were caught up just outside the lodge gates by Lady Bountiful, who also happened to be on her way to lunch with Mrs. Clancy.

At the luncheon party which ensued Mrs. French-Chichester was naturally in her element, and in excellent trim for being great friends with Nell, while at the same time making her thoroughly ineffective. She kept

the talk well in the groove of politics, upon
which topic Nell had nothing whatever to
say ; and triumphantly monopolized the good-
natured Lord Bridistow, who hardly got a
chance of saying a word to his beautiful young
hostess.

Meanwhile Sir Raby Pigott was pom-
pously testing—with much skill and aplomb,
as he imagined—the political soundness of
young Clancy. He found Terence a charm-
ingly modest young fellow, not too clever,
evidently willing to be guided by older and
wiser people, and with such a genuine Tory
bias as would do credit to any English
gentleman of the fine old school.

The widow enjoyed Terence's delicious
hypocrisy to the full, vowing to herself that she
had never appreciated him at his true worth
until to-day. Nell bore up against it as best
she could, accepting with quiet dignity her
rôle as a nonentity, a woman whose duty con-
sists of looking pretty and holding her tongue.

Terence and Mrs. French-Chichester were both really brilliant in their respective ways, insomuch that both haply regretted the mental poverty of their audience. No wonder, she reflected with a sigh, Terence was athirst for a larger world when here he had to pare down his wit in order to be understood at all.

After luncheon the gentleman adjourned to the billiard-room, nominally with a view to a game ; but the shrewd widow felt tolerably sure that the two guests intended to pocket something better than billiard-balls.

Being really excited and anxious, she was unable to sit still, and was glad to walk out on to the terrace with Nell. As they strolled up and down near the sun-dial, or leaned against the stone balustrade for a look at the terrace below and the green levels of the old formal garden, she amused herself by lecturing the young wife further upon the duties of her new station, and all the social procedure necessary for the securing of Terence's political position.

Nell listened meekly enough ; being somewhat ashamed at her own want of enthusiasm, yet vaguely hoping that time would bring her to a better frame of mind. She was aware that the elder lady despised her as a spiritless sort of creature, but was not analytical enough to perceive that her chief failing in the eyes of this critic was something which even time and patience would not amend—her scrupulous honesty. In fact, Nell and her husband, and their present adviser, lived on three separate ethical planes, the highest and lowest of which were too far apart for convenient intercourse. Nell, on the upper level, followed honesty as a guiding star ; Mrs. French-Chichester pursued self-interest no less unswervingly, and would admit no other motive into her calculations ; while Terence sympathized with both, and took a wavering course between them.

" I do wish we could put a little life into you, Nell; you're just as dull as this October day, or the old garden with its tiresome stiffness, its atmosphere of dead-and-gone hope, and churchyard quietude." Thus Nell's visitor wound up her lecture when some half-hour had passed without a sign from the men.

Yet the old garden, if sombre, looked quaint and interesting; and the weather was well enough for October, showing pearly gleams of light upon mellowing woods, and gauzy mists creeping up from the combe below.

At length, however, by the time Nell and her visitor were heartily tired of one another, the subtle scent of havannahs stole upon the air of the terrace; the gentlemen were coming round the corner of the house.

In a moment Mrs. French-Chichester read victory in their faces, and composed herself to accept it with proper simplicity of aspect.

Lord Bridistow and Sir Raby were beaming with complaisant satisfaction. Terence wore a deprecating, modest expression; but the pose of his figure, the very planting of his feet, betrayed to one keen observer that he had just accepted a proffered honour, and that his brain was now aglow with triumph.

As soon as he caught sight of the ladies, Lord Bridistow came forward with the frank *bonhomie* of a schoolboy to tell the story of the compact just completed, and forecast a brilliant career for their future member, Terence Clancy. Even pompous Sir Raby was talkative and excited.

Meanwhile Terence modestly detached himself from the group, and, resting upon the terrace balustrade, turned his face to the climbing oak woods across the combe, and, as the rich promise of the future gathered form and shape, allowed the smile of his heart to pass into his eyes. On his left was the old sun-dial, whose carved inscription had spoken to so many generations of the ancient Bampfylde family.

"*Scis horas, nescis horam,*" muttered Terence, as he glanced towards it. "Ah, but I *do* know the hour. The hour has come. The tide of my affairs has already been taken at the flood."

His gaze wandered away again to the steep oak coppice and downwards to where the tall ashes and alders, which marked the course of the hidden brook, were cut by the line of the garden wall. Presently the whole scene faded again, giving place to fancy-pictures of nobler line and hue; then something recalled him to earth again suddenly. In the boundary wall below him there was a dainty little wrought-iron gate, arched with stone chevrons, and giving access to a woodland path which led past the stables to some cottages higher up the combe. It was the opening of this gate that arrested his attention.

It surprised Terence a little to see the gate opened at all, for the stable people were not allowed to pass that way. But his first surprise quickly gathered force, and was merged in a vague consternation, when a familiar figure, which he had never learned to face without a quickened pulse, came slowly through the narrow opening and halted, looking upwards towards the terrace.

The figure supported itself for a few moments against one of the gate-piers, then advanced a few steps, then halted once more, as though unable to move more than a few yards at a time.

In this manner the intruder passed over a narrow strip of lawn and reached the broad gravel sweep leading up to the terrace steps. Terence watched him with a sickness of heart that deepened with each tottering effort which brought the man one step nearer.

" What has he come for ? Why has he

come in by the little gate ?" he muttered,
making a strenuous effort to brace up his
will and think coherently.

Some corner of the questioner's mind
answered promptly, "He has driven into
the stable-yard and been told that you are
on the terrace, and so has made his way
hither by the shortest route. He has come
to say that he has found you out. He is
half dead, by the look of him, but with life
enough left in him to ruin yours. Doidge
has you in his grasp at last, and will crush
you to powder."

"*Scis horas, nescis horam.*" The old sun-
dial seemed to be repeating the words in a
mocking whisper.

The talk and laughter of the group close
by were drifting to Terence's ears as though
from a distance ; compliments and congratu-
lations were buzzing behind him, ruin slowly
approaching him in front.

He still leaned heavily upon the balustrade,

incapable of movement; but the power of clear thought was coming back to him, and, for the first time, a perfect realization of his situation was shaping itself in his mind. He perceived that were his enemy in possession of the truth—and Ezekiel's face, now that he was drawing nearer, left hardly a vestige of doubt on this head—his social ruin was more absolute than he had ever yet imagined. He had driven Simon out of the country; he stood in Simon's shoes, in the full enjoyment of Simon's inheritance. Not a human soul would believe that he had drifted gradually into this position, without one thought of scheming his friend's downfall; that the stream of circumstance had carried him along, in spite of himself; that Fate had been too strong for him; that he had been always a weak drifter, but never a treacherous plotter — he must needs stand convicted in the eyes of all—worst of all, in Nell's eyes—as a most ignoble betrayer, not only of an innocent man, but of a friend and benefactor. He could not bear that—could not even begin to bear it; he could not stand upright for a moment under the storm of contumely that was about to burst over his head. The torture would kill him, unless—unless——

He turned his head for a moment, and cast one miserable glance backwards.

Nell was looking towards him, flushed and happy, with affectionate pride in her eyes. She had been listening to his praises —was already explaining away what seemed like hypocrisy in him, by saying to herself, "That was but a pretence put on to try me. He does in reality think with these gentlemen, and will serve their interests loyally."

His wife's bright looks seemed to revive Terence's drooping courage for the moment.

"I'm a coward," he muttered—"a weak, cringing coward. What proof against me can he possibly have obtained?"

But once more that corner of the mind which had apparently taken charge of him, and was ordering him about like a master, answered his question without hesitation— " When you rode over the town bridge an hour or two back, your enemy was among the loungers who watched you pass. And who was standing beside Doidge ? Some one you failed to recognize; but you stared at him—the short, hook-nosed man with the long beard—as though he were half familiar. Ah, it is dawning upon you—you recollect him well enough now. That was the man who sold you the pearl ring—your gift to Mary Pethick—the one Doidge kept among his relics. Don't cheat yourself by catching at straws—drown at once ; down with your head, and have done with it. See, your study window's open ; you have pluck enough to cheat your enemy yet. You have but to cross this narrow strip of gravel, pass through the open window, and pull out a drawer—you know which—then let them rave their loudest, you'll never hear them!"

Ezekiel had by this time reached the steps giving access to the lower terrace, and again halted, clinging for support to a carved stone vase. His victim could read his face now, clear as print, and the tale might be summed up in the one word—"ruin."

Once more Terence turned his despairing eyes to the group on his left. The two men and Mrs. French-Chichester were gazing surprisedly at the approaching figure; but in Nell's face there was something greater than surprise. He saw, or thought he saw, a growing horror of expectation, as though his former half-confession had suddenly grown complete.

It was the last straw to poor weak Terence; he could not face the coming torture. He thrust himself from the stone balustrade, and bent his wavering steps towards the study window. Nell took a step forward, as though with the intention of intercepting him, but got no further than the sun-dial, against which she leaned, staring wildly at the intruder.

Upon seeing his enemy disappear from the terrace above, Ezekiel uttered a low, harsh cry, and began to drag himself up the last flight of steps. By the time he had reached the terrace level, Terence was entering the open study window.

Doidge stood pointing after him, his face black with passion, his arm and body quivering.

The moment afterwards Terence saw the others close round him. Doidge's square figure was concealed behind the two tall gentlemen, and Terence seemed to hear the burning words wherewith his enemy was denouncing him. He stepped further into the room and disappeared.

Yet not a word was spoken—not a syllable escaped Ezekiel's lips. His cry from the lower terrace was the last sound he was ever to utter. His soul, at the very moment of discharging its load of vengeance, was claimed by Him whose office it would have usurped. The body which he had dragged so painfully to within a hand's-breadth of his goal sank, a lifeless, formless heap, upon the gravel terrace.

Even as they were bending over the dead Thing in awe and wonder, and Nell was kneeling pitifully beside it, with her hand straying towards the still heart, there was a loud report from the room behind them, and a wail from Nell proclaimed that the little drama had ended in a veritable tragedy.

CHAPTER IX.

"IS that you, Nell?"

"Yes. I am sitting here beside you."

A hard smile hovered in Terence's eyes as he turned them upon her, and his weak voice was full of bitterness.

"Sitting here beside me?" he muttered. "Yes; and passing a cruel judgment upon me, even as I expected. You've no mercy for me. You sit in judgment upon me, rehearsing all my faults, without a thought of forgiveness in your heart. We could never have gone on living together now that you've found me out, and I solemnly declare that it was the expectation of your merciless verdict on my sins that made me shoot myself. I'm glad I did it."

Terence was still lying in the study, on the sofa, where they had first laid him. He had shot himself in the breast, and was mortally wounded. He knew that his end was but a question of hours. As he had flatly declined to be moved upstairs, Jack Syme and the surgeon who had been summoned from Lymport by telegraph had done their best for him, and perforce acquiesced in his wishes.

Towards the two doctors and the servants who had assisted them Terence had shown his old gentleness of manner, praising their skill and thanking them for their care and pains; towards Nell alone he betrayed a bitterness of spirit such as shocked all those who witnessed it.

Good-natured Jack Syme had endeavoured to explain to Mrs. Clancy that her husband, though conscious, was really not himself, and had expressed a hope that, were he to sleep for an hour or two, he would, on re-awaking, return to his natural state. But the patient had now slept many hours, under the influence of morphia, and his feeling of repulsion towards his wife remained unaltered.

Nor did Nell seem overwhelmed by this unnatural attitude of his ; for her own mental state was too strange to permit of much resentment at his alienation. He had made no confession ; and none seemed needful. She seemed to know all from the moment when Ezekiel Doidge stood pointing after him from the top of the terrace steps. Nor could she quite grasp the fact that Terence was really upon his death-bed. The discovery of his incredible duplicity had, as it were, inundated her consciousness, submerging all other things, whether in the nature of fact or fancy. She had lost the power of realizing anything external to this

black discovery; and could only reiterate
again and again the miserable items of the
story, the manifold lies he had told her, his
deliberate, long-continued insistence upon
Simon's guilt, his cozening of Simon's friends
into that belief. Terence had so shocked
her out of her normal self that for the time
she could hardly believe in her own identity.

But after some time a terrible self-re-
pulsion took possession of Nell, a blank
despair at her own hardness.

"They tell me he can hardly live through
the night," she whispered many times over
as she watched beside him, "yet I don't
seem able to believe it. He's going to leave
me for ever, yet I can only harp and harp
upon his baseness. Am I going mad, or am
I the hardest and wickedest wife that ever
condemned an erring husband?"

After the few words above mentioned
there was dead silence in the dimly lighted
room. The husband and wife, upon whom

was already concentrated the talk of an amazed and horrified district, were apparently sundered so absolutely that the grave could not part them further.

The whole story was now perfectly well known, for Ezekiel had sent his witness on to Bickington, in accordance with his promise, after the identification of Clancy at the bridge. Immediately thereupon he had himself made straight for Monks Damerel, doubtless possessed by an insane fear lest his revenge should be snatched from him by Captain Rush ; and, but for a prolonged fainting-fit at the mill, he must have reached his destination almost as soon as Terence and his two guests.

Upon learning the news of Terence's identification, Captain Rush had himself galloped over to the hall, hoping to anticipate poor crazy Doidge and save Terence from the disgrace of a public exposure ; but he had only arrived to find that all was over.

Afterwards he had pushed on to Moor Gates, and rapidly driven Kate back to Monks Damerel, though, as Nell declined to see even her sister, this well-considered step had been of no avail.

But Nell and Terence gave no thought to what might be going on in the outer world; their own despair was like a dark eddy, round which they were being whirled with deadened hearts, unable to move hand or foot—face to face, yet with a gulf between that neither could cross.

When Terence at length broke the silence his strange bitterness seemed to be pricking him like a goad.

"How long is it since Syme left me? How long have I been asleep or unconscious?"

"Many hours! It is now midnight, or close upon it."

"I suppose you have spent all these hours in reckoning up my misdeeds, in comparing me, the sinner, with that immaculate hero-saint of yours, whom I hate now more than ever? Ah! I see by your face that I've guessed aright. I knew well enough what kind of mercy to expect from a virtuous woman. I say again that it is your spotless virtue that has killed me. With a wife more human and merciful, who could have made allowance and tempered judgment with human kindness, I might have repented and confessed long ago. You led me astray with your beauty first—for I loved poor Mary, and never dreamed of evading my solemn promise to her. Yes, but for you, I should have made her my wife, and we should have been happy. I've never been happy with *you*. I never could hope to live up to your crushingly superior level. I repeat, your beauty first led me astray, and then your virtue kept me astray, scaring me into one deception after another. I had to go on lying to save myself from your scorn.

Nor did you ever really love me ; you had
for me only a kind of spurious affection bred
of the desire to free yourself from an irksome
tie.   Had I ever possessed your love—such
love as a woman is capable of, and such as
poor Mary gave me—I should have made
a clean breast of it long ago.   Curious, isn't
it, that this parting scene of ours should be
bringing out the truth like this ?   And not
only do I see the past very clearly now, but
I also foresee the future.   I know precisely
what is coming, perceive it as clearly as
though it were actually happening before
my eyes."

These last sentences might have given
Nell the key to her husband's evil mood, but
she was herself too distracted to see through
his ravings.   Every word he said—for he
seemed to speak quietly and naturally, being
too weak to raise his voice—was to her
absolute truth ; and she could hardly breathe
under the heavy weight of his condemnation.

She sank upon her knees besides him, moaning, " I am a bad, hard woman, Terence; no condemnation of yours can be worse than that passed by myself. It is true that I have been going over your faults, that I don't seem able to forgive you. There's no power left me, I believe, but that of merciless judgment."

Then Terence began to groan and writhe with the pain, which had left him for a time, to return now with trebled force, and Nell went sobbing into the other room to fetch the doctor. Syme returned with her at once, drugged the suffering man off to sleep again, and once more left them together.

Nell once more took her place beside the couch, but not the same place. She sat close to it now, with her hand resting upon the coverlet near to her husband's. Her mind was entering upon a new phase, her spirit drawing nearer to his unconscious one, and a strange pitiful love was beginning to flutter in her heart.

She trembled with fear lest this apparent return to her better self should prove but a passing mood; but time went by and it still held good.

When Terence awoke, his expression was changed; he, too, seemed different, as though her spirit had been working upon his, or as though both had passed under some soothing mysterious influence, been softened by some "sweet oblivious antidote."

"It was terrible to see you in such pain, Terence. I'm thankful to know that it has passed away again."

Terence's hand moved a few inches and lay beside hers, touching, though not holding it.

"Yes, the pain has left me, Nell; and when it returns you can yourself measure out the morphia, for I want no one else to interrupt us. There is no need to call Jack

Syme in. I will tell you exactly what to do. Nell, we must make an effort to wrestle down the barrier that's between us. There's a conflict before us, yet I feel that we may yet attain to peace before we part. Let me know now what Doidge said; tell me the exact words in which he denounced me."

"He spoke no word—not a syllable, Terence."

He gazed at her incredulously, but her pale solemn face was a clear assurance that she had no thought of deceiving him.

"What can have tied his tongue? I read my ruin in his face. He would never have spared me of his own free will. What can have hindered his revenge?"

"I firmly believe that he was called away to some better task."

Nell spoke in a clear low voice, with the reverence of one who touches upon some holy mystery.

"Do you mean that he's dead?" groaned

Terence. "Nell, Nell, his blood is upon my head! I might have saved him. The aneurism must have burst. I always knew he had it, and I never made an effort to save him. No one else knew it. His life was entrusted to me, do you see? and I let him die rather than risk the discovery of my secret. Nell, take your hand from mine, I'm not fit to touch you. I know myself all through now, and find no clean spot in my soul. I did think I had been honest in my profession, but even there I am stained—stained; there's no hope for one so base, so stained!"

Nell knelt beside her husband and wept over him. His despair called forth all the love and mercy in her heart; and he wept with her like a child.

"I must tell you all now, Nell—*all;* and then you'll surely turn from me again."

Then he poured forth the story of his long duplicity—with truth and candour, and a power of self-judgment that had never come to him before; and the bad black Thing that Nell had shuddered at was now seen, not as a great dominating carved figure of treachery, but rather as a strange pathetic one of human weakness—a mournful shape, built up piece by piece, moulded by the unwilling hand of a workman who had many, many times turned from his task, loathing it and himself, yearning often to shatter it to fragments, but too weak to destroy his own miserable handiwork.

"That's *all*," he concluded; "that's the story of my life since I first knew you; and the moral of it is sad enough—that kind feeling and good intentions go for nothing, worse than nothing, without principle and will to back them. You know the worst of me now, Nell, and I can pass into the other state free from the burden of any secret. But I fear you will turn?"

No, Nell did not turn from him now.

Sacred tears fell upon his face, his wife's lips
met his, breathing tenderness and yearning
pity.

"Nell, my own love, what can have
possessed me to say those cruel things to
you a while back ?   I scarce know ; a demon
seemed to possess me.   Ah, but I do know,
and I'll tell it out straight and plain, for sure
I've had enough of covering up my sins !
The demon was just jealousy.   I felt that
you were unforgiving, and that was torture ;
but something rankled deeper—the thought
that my degradation was *his* elevation, that
you were longing for *him*, making a martyr
of him, setting him up once more upon his
pedestal, while I sank lower and lower.   I've
always been more jealous of him than even
you imagined; even now I can't bear to·
mention his name.   Yes, jealous always.
Truth is truth, and I declare I hated him
the more for the benefits he heaped upon
me.   'Jealousy cruel as the grave?'   Ay,

and perhaps outlasting it, and verily 'the coals thereof are coals of fire.' . . . But, my love, never give another thought to those jealous ravings of mine—lies, all lies, I say. Your superiority, which I railed at, so far from hurting me, saved me from complete degradation, kept my conscience alive. I've never been quite free from remorse; half my late ambition sprang from the desire to stifle it. Sweet wife, kiss me forgiveness of those lies. . . . Ah, Nellie, you're a good and loving woman!" After a pause he added, "Think how I can best atone to you for those ravings, sweetheart."

"Do not think of me now, Terence; but —but surely an atonement is due to—to some one else?"

Terence understood her clearly, and the light went from his face; he had not exaggerated the power of his jealousy.

"*You* can tell him, Nell—that man, I mean—that I am sorry."

"No one knows whither he has gone; I may never see him again."

"Say that again; it comforts me to hear it. I trust and hope you never will see him again—never!"

"And remember, Terence, that he bore public disgrace for our sake. Surely, oh, surely, there should be public atonement?"

"Would you have the parson preach out my shame from the pulpit? You know well enough that the whole neighbourhood will be ringing with my wickedness and his noble generosity—won't that be enough for you?"

"Oh, Terence, you disappoint me. Surely at this solemn time you must be willing to make whatever reparation lies in your power?"

"I'm dying with a load of shame on my name—isn't that reparation enough? If he's as grand and magnanimous as you've always made out, that will satisfy him, I should think; especially as he'll come back, as I know well—and the knowledge is a worse torture than the pain I've been through—to claim *you !*"

She drew away without a word, and a burning blush covered her pale face.

" Nell, Nell, 'tis a shame to hurt you so, but that's what will happen, unless——— Listen, now. You urge me to a self-sacrifice that tastes very bitter. I wonder if you desire this so much as to be willing to match it with one of your own ? "

" I would do anything to give you ease of mind and cure this terrible craze that possesses you."

" Would you—would you ? If I undertook to make the reparation you desire, would you promise me on your honour never to speak to Simon again, to avoid even seeing him, to leave the neighbourhood should he ever return ? "

" Must I never even thank him for all he has gone through for my sake ? " she asked, weeping.

" You may write to him once. Put your thanks into one letter, and have done with him and the whole matter for ever ; then I think I could die in peace."

For some moments there was no sound in the room but that of Nell's sobs, which gradually ceased.

When she leaned over him again she was dry-eyed and deadly pale ; and Terence put his arms about his wife's neck, knowing without a word that he had won his desire.

" My own dear love," he whispered, " have I asked too much of you ?"

Her face quivered, but he saw that she was steadfastly bent upon making the compact and keeping it. Then the power of her self-abnegation entered into Terence's soul like a fire, and burned away at last the

mean jealousy that darkened it. With his
arms still round her, his heart answering to
hers, and with a strange exaltation in his
feeble voice, he murmured —

" Darling, you conquer me utterly. Most
true and noble wife, I'm not so base as I
believed. A weak and erring man, but not
so base as to make your pain the price of
my right-doing. God forbid that I should
fetter you so! Oh, Nell, Nell, you're free,
my own love, absolutely free! I'll have no
compact with you—I'll make that reparation
of my own free will ; and God bless you for
shaming me into doing my duty! My love,
the torture's coming again. Listen, for my
strength's failing. Tell the vicar all, and let
him make my story public as he thinks best.
. . . Sweetheart, kiss me once more, and
don't weep so, darling. . . . And remember
always that I loved you—remember that, for
'tis the only thing to set against my faults.
I love you, I love you—' unto the last gasp,

darling.' Who was it said those words? I cannot remember now, but let me repeat them as my own—'unto the last gasp, darling!'"

CHAPTER X.

THERE is no commoner or more conventional phrase than that which describes any given community as being "like one man;" and in the case of Chillington, when the story of Secretan's self-sacrifice and Clancy's duplicity spread through the little community, any one man, almost, might have been picked out to give voice to the sentiments of all.

The town and neighbourhood, in fact, received the news very much as any ordinary person of average goodness of heart might have been expected to do. There was first a strong wave of indignation against the real

culprit, together with a desire to make
amends to the man who had suffered wrongly,
whether by his own fault or not. For some
eight and forty hours this mixed feeling held
sway; then came the news of Terence
Clancy's death, and with it a tendency to
qualify judgment with mercy. For the
ancient sentiment which forbids a man to
speak ill of a dead brother is rooted deeply
in the soil of human nature; and, though
tending somewhat towards injustice to the
living—since man would seem to have a
certain quantum of judging-energy in his
system which must be worked off in some
direction or other—is doubtless good at the
core. At any rate, when the young squire
of Monks Damerel died, the voice of condemnation took a gentler tone, and a profound curiosity as to the rights of the whole
matter took possession of the town.

It was understood that Mr. Nelson, the
vicar, had been requested by the dying man

to make the whole story known, and it was expected that he would do so from the pulpit. But for reasons of his own the vicar preferred to discharge his trust in a manner separate from his office; and, as Clancy's death entailed a new general meeting of the cricket club, he made it known that the opportunity would be availed of for saying what was necessary for the purpose.

When the day came round, and all the neighbourhood was once more gathered in the ancient town hall, Mr. Nelson came forward and quietly made his statement. He explained that he wished to speak as a friend to his friend, not as a pastor to his flock, since his own judgment had erred in common with theirs. They had all alike assumed silence under accusation to be synonymous with guilt.

After which prologue he told the story in brief plain terms, putting forward no comments of his own, drawing no deductions, pointing no moral, but allowing the facts of the case to speak for themselves. He was listened to amidst an impressive silence.

Afterwards Lord Bridistow rose to his feet and requested the chairman's permission to make a suggestion. It was to the effect that Sir Simon Secretan should be enrolled as their new captain.

"For though it would be but a small step to take," the speaker continued, "I think it would be a step in the right direction. We've wronged the man, and I think we ought to show our sense of having done so. I don't pretend to any better right of judgment than any one of you; I don't even know whether my friend was right or wrong in allowing us to misjudge him so. Perhaps his conduct was Quixotic and over-strained, and that sort of thing; but I do think there's a spice of nobility to be found somewhere in it; and I do believe we want a few more such Quixotes just to show us what poor old human nature is still capable of. I don't know where my friend Secretan is. None of us know that. His solicitor, even, is not allowed to know his address, but conducts his affairs through another agent at the Cape. Yet I suppose we can convey to him the news of our decision, and that simple message will suffice to show our wish to welcome him among us again. And, gentlemen, I do believe that if he ever comes back we shall understand our Quixote better, be ready to accept him as one who practises as much, nay more, than he ever preached. I think, though he failed in many of his schemes, he has now succeeded in one thing —that is, in educating us up to the point of comprehending a man made of somewhat finer stuff than ourselves."

Sir Simon Secretan was elected accordingly, with every sign of grave approval, but without applause or further discussion, for the shadow of a recent tragedy hung heavily over the gathering. It seemed but a few days since poor Terence had poured forth his wit and drollery from that platform, and most of those present were glad that a complete revelation of his wrong-doing permitted them to still think kindly of their favourite of yesterday.

This quiet and subdued public meeting was the only event that broke the routine life of Chillington for a considerable time. Ezekiel Doidge's mill, together with all his other property, was sold under the terms of his will, and the son of a Lymport tradesman reigned in his stead. Mr. Tredethlyn and his two daughters had gone abroad, and it was understood that they were not expected home again for a twelvemonth or more. The hall at Monks Damerel was in the hands of a caretaker; Moor Gates was let by the month to a family whose respectable dulness tended rather to intensify the stagnation of the neighbourhood. Under which circumstances Mrs. French-Chichester fought for some months against a steadily growing depression, then shut up the Manor House and vanished London-wards—just in time, as she herself declared, to escape suicide.

Meanwhile, Chillington wasted much curious speculation upon the question of Sir Simon's return, until, no sign or hint of such a probability being published, even that topic lost interest, leaving the weather, the crops, and the state of trade once more to reign supreme.

When the spring came round again, however, a slight breeze of interest sprang up from an unexpected quarter—the direction of Bickington Park.

It was rumoured that the pottering old squire, whose existence was apt to be almost forgotten during his son's absence, was about to become a speculator in house-building. He was going to erect a dozen or more big mansions along the eastern fringe of the property ; thus making a kind of fashionable suburb for Chillington, to be occupied mainly by summer visitors from Lymport—in short, a desirable inland health-resort.

This report held the public ear and the commercial mind of Chillington for some weeks, when the looked-for suburb dwindled to a mere brace of buildings ; and, finally, even that pair of mansions collapsed, leaving but a gamekeeper's lodge to stem the tide of a thwarted town's indignation.

Yet things were in reality not quite so bad as this ; for the squire of Bickington did actually contemplate the erection of a large country house ; not in the direction of the town, but away on the further verge of his property, a narrow strip of which reached down to the left bank of the Culmer river.

He had not as yet quite made up his mind to the step ; and, curiously enough, the final decision of the matter rested with Miss Tredethlyn. Not that, as the whole district presently concluded, she was about to marry the squire's son—for that affair has not as yet progressed beyond the point where we last left it—but for reasons that can easily be set forth.

Briefly, then, it must be explained that Captain Saunderson had by this time so far recovered his health as to feel equal to supporting the rigours of his native climate ; and, further, was possessed by a craving, surprising in so delicate a man, to resume the robust sports and pastimes proper to an Englishman. In fact, he was heartily sick of continental lounging, and had joyfully made up his mind to settle at home.

Now, as an ardent Nimrod, he naturally had hankerings after Leicestershire ; but honest Mrs. Saunderson had other views, and by judicious handling gently led him to follow the same, while seeming only to be following his lead. For in truth, being a humble woman at the core, she had misgivings as to her reception in the county society for which she thirsted.

" My dear John," as she herself put it with a *naïveté* that no foreign travel could obliterate, "advertisement is the soul of modern life ; without it you can't plant a new thing upon the market, anyway. Well, I'm a new thing to society, and maybe not a very high-class article neither—' seventeen under proof when bottled,' as we used to say ; and advertisement is what I need. Just as you go to the doctor's to certify the excellence of a new whisky or gin, so must you go to people in society to advertise, and answer for, *me*. Now, if we go and pitch our tent in a new county, you'll be free to hunt your fill, no doubt, but who'll call on your wife, I should like to know ? Whereas, if you take a place in the Chillington district, with my nieces and some of their friends to give me a lift, happen I'll do well enough. You'll get hunting there, too, and salmon-fishing in

the Culmer, as well as heaps of shootin'—
and my people at Lymport won't never inter-
fere with us.   I'll answer for that."

Thus it fell upon a day that Captain
Saunderson and his wife drove up to the
Falcon Hotel at Chillington, with the avowed
object of spending a week or two in exploit-
ing the neighbourhood; whereupon Squire
Rush, with the intuition of true genius, at
once perceived the possibilities of the situation.   Julius, as luck would have it, was away
soldiering in Ireland at this time, so this
deep schemer was perfectly free to work out
his plots.

Accordingly, the first thing he did was to
install the Saundersons at Bickington Park,
and to drive them all round the neighbourhood house-hunting.   This continued until
they had inspected every bit of brick and
mortar on the books of the local house-agents ;
but, alas ! the search was vain—there was
nothing vacant at all likely to suit them.

The squire's spirits sank low; but he rallied swiftly, and resolved upon a stroke at once subtle and bold.

First, however, he deemed it advisable to write confidentially to Miss Tredethlyn at Bordighera, with a view to sounding her concerning the proposed scheme, for it was necessary to know clearly how she was likely to receive the seventeen-under-proof aunt as a neighbour.

Kate's reply happened to be satisfactory ; and with that letter crushed in his pocket, Mr. Rush stepped up to his two guests and roundly offered to build a house for them of any size and shape and style they might desire. That was how the new mansion on the lip of the Culmer vale came into existence.

The Tredethlyns returned from the Continent soon after the installation of Captain and Mrs. Saunderson in their new home, when Kate at once set about giving a loyal support to Aunt Mary's efforts towards making of herself an article suitable for planting upon the social market.

Nor did the task prove so severe as Kate had anticipated. Money is money, whether poured from the mouth of a vulgar gin-bottle, or emanating from the breeches-pocket of the noblest of Norman ancestors ; and Kate found it to contain a power of enlarging a neighbourhood's charity, such as no human rhetoric could possess. Mrs. French-Chichester came and assisted her zealously; and the gradual, perhaps painful, process of social establishment to which expectation had pointed, turned out to be no more than an easy slide down an inclined plane.

The Machiavel of Bickington watched the proceedings meanwhile from the standpoint of a benevolent spectator ; noted with deep satisfaction the growing intimacy between Moor Gates and Culmer Lodge, as the new place was called, and slyly bided his time.

The Saundersons mounted their establishment in the early summer, and were firmly
planted in the social soil by the middle of
autumn. Julius was to be home for his two
months' leave about Christmas time, when
the squire's plan must either be brought to
a triumphant conclusion or finally dropped ;
for Mr. Rush had made up his mind that,
were his soldier son to return to Ireland
once more a free unscathed bachelor, he
might as well give up his pet scheme in
despair.

In due time Captain Rush came home, and
the squire's suspense reached the feverish
stage. The hunting season was in full swing,
the weather open, and Julius appeared to
have no thought beyond the pleasures of the
chase. But after some hopeless weeks, a
cheering frost in, and once more the squire's
courage revived.

Having seen a good deal of Captain
Saunderson in the hunting-field, Julius

naturally became a frequent visitor at Culmer Lodge as soon as the frost put an end to sport ; and, as he came and went, the private league against the doomed man's freedom was working constantly and subtly. Aunt Mary could never get through a week without having dear Kate over to enliven her, and was always getting up some little dance or other entertainment for dear Kate's benefit ; Captain Saunderson was under strict orders to press his intimacy with Julius ; to the squire was assigned the task of keeping Julius thoroughly well bored of home. In a word, between three or four of them, the stubborn bachelor was successfully immeshed.

In truth, Captain Rush was a very willing victim ; and the presence of Kate's homely relative appeared to have just the soothing effect upon his pride which his father had anticipated. He slid smoothly into a picturesque kind of intimacy with Miss Tredethlyn, an easeful relation such as permitted them to show one another those good qualities which they had formerly been at such pains to conceal ; and so gradually the barrier between them was worn thinner and thinner, until his attentions became those of a real suitor ; after which he was too proud a man to withdraw, even if intimacy had lessened liking, which was far from being the case. Thus it came about one night, on the occasion of a dance at Culmer Lodge, that these tiresome young people, who had given their friends such a deal of unnecessary trouble and anxiety, sank their pride to the betrothal point ; and the squire hardly slept for two nights afterwards.

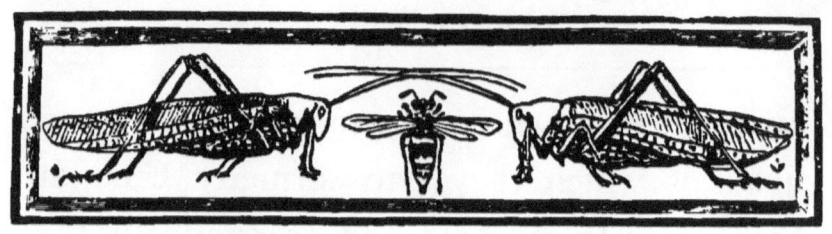

CHAPTER XI.

"MY dear Kate, allow me to state that this son and heir of mine is shockingly spoiled."

"I believe you're right, Julius; and I think no one has contributed to this disastrous state of things more than yourself."

"Tut—tut, you libel me! Why, every one knows what a stern parent I am?"

"Your wife has yet to acquire that piece of knowledge, however."

Kate had her little son in her arms, and was watching her husband finish his breakfast; and a very handsome, proud, happy young mother she looked. If the courtship

of this young couple had consisted of alter-
nate storm and gloom, it was tolerably
evident that their three years of married
life had been of quite another complexion.

" I repeat," persisted Julius, pushing back
his chair and opening his newspaper, " that
this young scamp is a positive disgrace to
us ; and the only question is—who is to bear
the blame ? "

" Suppose we agree to put it all upon the
squire, Julius ? You might call him in at
once—I saw him pass down the greenhouse
not five minutes since—and read him a filial
lecture on the spot. It might have a good
effect ;upon this boisterous youth, whom I
shall endeavour to keep quiet for the first time
in his life while the lecture's proceeding."

" Very good ! " said Julius, " I'll follow
your suggestion ; for the truth is, my father
has got somewhat out of hand lately. He is
not kept in nearly such good order as my
troop used to be. I'll call him in at once."

· "Call who in, dear lad ? " asked the squire himself, stepping through the door which communicated with the greenhouses on this side.

"The Squire of Bickington," Julius answered, looking sternly at his father. "And it is my duty to speak seriously to the old gentleman. I am given to understand that he has been found aiding and abetting a fond mother, and a brace of foolish nurses, in the demoralization of that youngster yonder. I can call half a dozen witnesses to prove his guilt, and my intention is to make a severe example of him. What have you to say, sir, in defence of this misguided grandfather ? "

For a moment the old squire stood holding the door-handle, and regarding his son with a scared and puzzled expression ; then a sly smile wrinkled his face, and a gentle chuckle ensued.

"Have you instituted these proceedings

against me, Kate? How dare you set one criminal to try another? I'll rob you of that little wretch for a whole morning if you go a-plotting against an old man so; or stay, give me over the precious little lad at once, and I may forgive you this time."

" The fact is," said Kate, with a proud smile at her husband, " we are such an unhappy couple that we're forced to sink our differences sometimes by an assault upon a third party. Little Julius won't come to you—see !"

Little Julius, in fact, sent up a powerful roar by way of protest against the suggested exchange, and had to be propitiated by the hasty offer of some half-dozen light articles ; after throwing which upon the floor one after another, he cheered up so far as to consent to be perched upon his grandfather's shoulder for a space.

" There—now that we've settled our dif-ferences," said the old man, beaming upon his son and daughter, "I'll tell you both a secret. There's an interesting letter for Kate in my coat pocket."

"From whom?"

"Ah, that's just what you're dying to know, as I'm quite aware; but I'm going to sell my news. Now listen, you promise to lend me this little chap and his nurse for an hour's drive this afternoon, and I'll tell you?"

"Is it from the Cape?" asked Kate, eagerly. "Has Simon written at last?"

"The letter's from London, so don't excite yourself about nothing, my dear. Why should Simon write? He has forgotten us all long ago. Why, how long is it since he left home?"

"How old is Young Hopeful?" asked the boy's father.

"One year, nine months, and five days, at six o'clock this morning," answered the grandfather promptly.

" Then Simon has been an exile a little over four years."

" He'll leave his bones in a foreign land, be very sure of that," the squire continued, slyly bestowing a lump of sugar upon Young Hopeful.

" Give me the letter, please."

" Give me your promise first, my dear Kate ? "

" You shall have the boy from two till half-past."

" From two till three, or you never see your letter ! "

The squire held up the missive enticingly, address downwards, and Master Julius promptly snatched it out of his hand. Whereupon Kate wheedled the letter from her son, and cried—

" Julius, look—look ! Simon's handwriting, and the London postmark ? "

" Posted by his solicitors, no doubt," Julius answered calmly.

"Is it, indeed?" Kate laughed excitedly as she tore open the letter. Then, after perusing a few lines, this dignified young matron began to dance round the room, crying, "He has come home—poor old Simon! and wants to know whether we should care to have him here for a few days—dear old Simon!—because he has no other friends in these parts to whom he cares to go. Oh, Julius, isn't it pitiful?"

"What's the matter now?" asked Julius, who always waxed provokingly cool when deeply interested. "Is the man homeless, or starving, that you must needs waste pity upon him?"

But Julius could not altogether conceal the fact that he, too, was excited. He and the squire devoured the letter over Kate's shoulder; and all three kept up a running fire of pleased comment as they did so.

"Well," concluded Julius, quickly recovering his usual phlegm, "you had better write to this returned exile in a day or two, though it's evident that he is not over keen about coming down here."

"Write in a day or two?" exclaimed his wife, indignantly; "wire this instant, you mean! Pray ring the bell, Julius, and don't be so abominably cool."

"You're welcome to get into a fume, Kate, without which no woman's happiness is complete; but I warn you that you'll be disappointed. Simon writes calmly, and talks of leaving the country again in a few weeks; and I've little doubt that such is his real intention. It's evident to me that he's wrapped up in this adopted daughter of his, and thinks of nobody else; that he has no idea of settling among us again and renewing old friendships. I notice an undertone of bitterness in his letter, and—— "

"Julius, will you have the kindness to adjourn to the stables, or go round the greenhouses with your father? You are only interrupting my household duties here, both of you."

Having thus got rid of her men kind, Kate despatched her telegram, and fell to ruminating.

Should she send a note over to Monks Damerel to acquaint Nell with this interesting news? No; she quickly decided to take no such step, though the temptation to do so was considerable. In fact, Kate had long ago thought out a policy to meet such an eventuality as this of Simon's return. Conscious of an intense desire to throw him and her sister together, she felt that any step she might take in that direction would only tend to defeat her own end. If Simon ever were minded to return to his old love, he should be left absolutely free. Any hint of leading or persuasion, any manipulation of circumstances, or smoothing of his path, might be fatal.

Nor was Kate at all certain as to her

sister's views on this subject. It had been tacitly agreed between them never to touch upon it. Even in their most confidential moments Simon's name was never mentioned.

On her return from the Continent the young mistress of Monks Damerel had naturally been the centre of much romantic interest and curiosity. A little stir was created when she first settled down at the hall with her father; after which there ensued a pause of expectation throughout the neighbourhood.

As a matter of course it was prophesied that Sir Simon Secretan would return in a year or two, and would quickly persuade Mrs. Clancy to once more change her name. The time went by, however, and this most symmetrical arrangement grew less and less probable; whereupon many other suitors began to cast sheep's eyes towards the beautiful young widow. Indeed, Nell had more opportunities of changing her condition than even this quick-eyed district was ever aware of. But a widow she remained, making no attempt to shut herself up from the world, yet apparently concerning herself very little about it.

On the whole, people were disappointed with Mrs. Clancy of Monks Damerel. They would have liked one extreme or the other; either a woe-begone young widow, living a life of deep romantic seclusion, and only exhibiting a pale interesting countenance to the world at large about once a year, or a dazzling young queen reigning triumphantly—and they got neither.

As the day wore on, and Kate received no reply to her pressing telegram, her excitement increased; for she began to think it probable that Simon would later in the day answer the message in person.

In the course of the afternoon there were a good many visitors to receive, and every fresh arrival gave her a thrill of expectation. Every moment, almost, she expected to hear Sir Simon Secretan announced.

But her drawing-room filled and emptied; routine talk buzzed on unflaggingly; and the commonplace decorum of the afternoon was unbroken by anything more dramatic than the announcement of a new engagement.

At length the cup-and-saucer parade was over, and Kate was free to pay a visit to the nursery. But hardly had she time to attract the notice of Young Hopeful, who chanced to be too busy destroying some new toys to concern himself about anything so unimportant as a fond mother, when she was informed of Simon's arrival.

Then Kate sailed downstairs and crossed the hall in a prodigious flutter. Could it really be their old friend Simon, who seemed to have forgotten their existence for four whole years? She felt an odd inclination to run away into the shrubbery, and put off the meeting for an hour or more; but she got into the drawing-room somehow, and there stood Simon, whose warm grasp of the hand quickly proved him to be a man of flesh and blood. For a moment or two Kate could only stare at him in silence; but the self-possession of the big bronzed man quickly restored to her the use of her tongue.

" Dear old Simon—why, how brown you are !"

After a separation of four years the remark seemed absurdly inadequate, and they both laughed heartily.

" Nice change in the weather, isn't it, Kate ?" he retorted, by way of keeping up the farce. But she promptly sat him down in an armchair, rang for some more tea, and told him not to talk nonsense.

Simon seemed to be changed for the better in many ways, though it took Kate a little time to appreciate this. He was less morbid and dreamy, and there was a wholesome ring in his cordial voice; it was apparent that change and travel had been a beneficial treatment for Timon of Chillington.

When the first excitement was over, and they had settled down to rational conversation, Kate found there was little to tell her visitor in the way of news. He had either kept himself posted up in the affairs of Chillington all the time he was abroad, or had so far lost interest in the place and neighbourhood as to lend an unwilling ear to all local news—Kate hardly knew which might be the true explanation. As for his own travels and adventures, he was ready enough to talk of them, as also of his adopted daughter and the progress of her education; and for some time Kate listened with interest to his recital.

Presently, however, a waft of nervous apprehension disturbed her; for in the midst of Simon's discourse she perceived, through the open window at his back, a person whom she certainly wished fifty miles away at this moment—her sister Nell.   She heartily wished now that she had warned Nell of this probable arrival, and so given her a chance of preparing for a meeting, the awkwardness of which would now be increased tenfold.   Still, on second thoughts, her policy of non-interference could not be other than a sound one—only it seemed rather hard on Nell just at present.

Meanwhile, Nell dawdled slowly across the lawn in an uncertain way which irritated her sister's tense nerves not a little; and Simon talked cheerfully on without the least suspicion that his listener was on tenterhooks.

As Nell drew near, her sister rose and walked to the window, hoping to warn her away by a gesture; but the former, upon catching sight of Kate, spoke at once, and then it was too late.

"What is the matter with you, Kate? You look as solemn and portentous as though—— "

"There's some one come to see us," said Kate, curtly.

Then Simon rose and walked to the window, and there was nothing more to be done.

Kate stared at them both in a perfectly imbecile fashion, and was unable to help out the awkward situation by a word.

But apparently no help was needed. Nothing could have been, at least on the face of it, more flat and commonplace than this meeting, which should have been a little romance in itself. Simon's opening remarks, for any sentiment they contained, might have been taken straight from a guide-book, and Nell at once fell into his vein. Their greetings resembled those of old acquaintances on a railway platform, who are willing to exchange civilities for a moment or two, but rather hope the arrival of their respective trains may cut them short.

Kate was inexpressibly disappointed.

"To think what he has gone through for her!" she muttered; "and now he won't allow her to thank him even by a glance. He declines even to receive a friendly word for her. She can do nothing in the face of such an iced manner as that. He's more bitter than I had imagined."

The scene was brief as well as commonplace; for, after staying just as long as propriety demanded, Simon excused himself by saying that he was anxious to meet Julius, who was expected home from the town about this hour, and strolled away towards the west lodge gate with that object in view.

Being thus left alone with Nell, Kate was almost afraid to look at her, yet withal was intensely curious to see how she would take this disappointment. Would Nell wax tearful and pathetic, or would she keep up her pretence of indifference ?

Nell was not long in showing the colour of her mood. As she stood looking after Simon, who was visible for some distance down the drive, she was panting with indignation, and presently exclaimed—

"It's a shame—a cruel shame to treat an old friend so! And it's not like him to show such unkindness and malice."

"*You* have no right to criticize him!" Kate retorted with some asperity.

"I thought—I did think——" continued Nell ; then she stopped abruptly.

"What do you think, Nell ? Come, I've never intruded upon your reserve in this connection, so you may as well reward me by making a clean breast of your sentiments. You needn't fear any interference on my part. I shall let you take your own course, whatsoever it may be. Nor could I hinder you, for the matter of that, for you always were a perfect model of obstinacy."

"My course will be no course at all!" cried the young widow, flashing another indignant glance after Simon's retreating figure; "for I will have nothing to do with a man who outrages me so. Kate, I'll tell you frankly what I had hoped!"

"No fear about the frankness, once you've let your tongue loose!" muttered Kate, parenthetically.

"I had hoped that when Simon returned it would be as an old friend; and—and I did hope he would give me some chance of showing my gratitude—and perhaps restoring at last what rightly belongs to him."

"Quite so—I see. That is pretty much the line I thought you would take, my dear. You want to marry him out of gratitude! So far, so good. Any love to be thrown in, may I ask?"

"I've done with all that long ago."

"Ah, just as I supposed! You're so old
and ugly now that any thought of romance
has now become an absurdity! Well, I
quite understand your scheme, Nell, and
I tell you at once that it won't do. You
want to give him your hand and purse, and
keep your heart to yourself. Now, it's quite
possible that he knows you well enough to
have made as near a guess at your intentions as I have done, and has put on coldness accordingly. Anyhow, it won't do.
You want to treat Simon as a shopman, to
whom you owe a good long bill, and for
whom you're therefore ready to make some
sacrifice, and he's not the man for that kind
of barter. Truly, it's a comical situation.
In the old days he wanted to marry you,
and you couldn't bring yourself to have him;
now you want to marry him, and he won't
accept you upon any consideration—at least,
judging from the first scene of the comedy.
You're, in fact, a brace of lunatics, as I

always said—a fatuous, high-flown, romantic, ridiculous, tiresome pair — and I'll have nothing whatever to do with you. Fight it out between yourselves by all means; I shan't stir a finger to help or hinder. Make him an offer through your solicitor, if it so please you, stating clearly what pin-money you propose to afford him, and explaining that you'll allow him every possible liberty, etc., provided that he's careful not to step beyond the limits of ordinary friendship."

" I shall do nothing of the sort, Kate; nor shall I even speak to him again except as a distant acquaintance. I shall avoid your house until he's gone—and if I do meet him in society——"

"Yes, yes—I know all about it, my dear child. Don't expend all this excitement upon me, for it is a mere waste of time. You won't stay and dine, of course ?"

" Is it likely ? "

" Not in the least. I only asked as a

matter of form. But, as the man will be back soon, and I must think about going up to dress, you had better depart in haste— and by the east lodge, or you might chance to come across Sir Ogre again!"

CHAPTER XII.

THE family at Bickington found no great difficulty in persuading Simon to extend his visit beyond the meagre seven days which he had originally named as its probable limit. In fact, the returned exile found the atmosphere of the neighbourhood far more congenial than he had expected.

Perhaps he had not sufficiently taken into consideration how greatly the change in public opinion towards himself would affect the question of his happiness; and had by no means realized how warming to the heart it is to be greeted with marked cordiality by a dozen old acquaintances every time one takes a walk into the town. Probably, also, he had feared to become an object of public curiosity; whereas he now found, to his profound relief, that not even the worst busybody in the place seemed moved to make any allusion to the past. But what surprised him most of all was that almost every one in the neighbourhood seemed glad to see him.

Simon's old friend, the Vicar of Chillington, hurried over to visit him the moment his arrival at Bickington was made known, and his long silent hand-clasp was worth many noisier greetings. Lord Bridistow followed almost at Frank Nelson's heels, welcomed Simon as a returning prodigal, and vowed to have him locked up if he ever talked of leaving the country again. Many others, too, came in the wake of these old friends; and Lord Bridistow had cause to repeat a former phrase of his, to the effect that Secretan had educated his public up to the point of understanding him. Certainly it did seem that Chillington had added a new item of knowledge to its general philosophy of human nature—namely, that a man who takes upon himself the burden of other people's troubles, and gives time and thought to their alleviation, is not necessarily a hypocrite or a fool.

Moreover, some of Lord Timon's old philanthropic schemes had fructified during these four years. A certain benefit society, which had once barely survived the shattering effects of Mr. Jackson's manipulation, was now in a flourishing condition. As for the farm hospital for the dying, that had from the first been a modest but complete success ; and the greater establishment at Lymport, built a couple of years afterwards by public subscription, undoubtedly owed its origin to Simon's experiment on a small scale at Hollacomb.

Concerning his latest experiment of all,

the guardianship of a young child, the general public were naturally little interested; but his friends at Bickington were very curious to see little Rose.

Thus, as soon as Simon decided upon extending his visit, it was requested that the child and her governess should be sent for from town—an arrangement upon which Julius Rush commented to his wife in this wise—

"You'll be glad enough to be rid of her in a week or two—for isn't one spoiled child scourge enough for one household?"

But, to the surprise of every one at Bickington Park, little Rose turned out to be under very good control—a bright and frolicsome child, but certainly better disciplined than Kate at all expected to find Master Julius at six years old.

Simon had always had a knack of refuting the prophecies of critical friends; but even Kate, who always expected a good deal of

him, was astonished at his latest achieve
ment.   She perceived that he must have
studied minutely the art of child-handling,
and have bestowed extraordinary care and
pains upon the bringing up of this little
person, for it was apparent, from the firm
hold he had obtained of his adopted daughter,
that he must have taken a considerable
personal share in her training and education.
"And probably," reflected Kate, who was
now naturally a student of the child question,
"the little one has been at the same time
unconsciously educating him."

At any rate, they were all agreed that
Rose was a piquante and attractive little
creature, and that the relations between the
child and her adopted father were of a quaint
and old-world fashion.

The end of three weeks found the pair
still domiciled at Bickington, though by this
time Simon showed signs of growing restive.
His four years of wandering seemed to have

unfitted him for settling down finally in any one spot, and their efforts to persuade the wanderer to cast anchor among his old friends seemed to fall upon deaf ears. But, though he continued to speak of his return to the other side of the world as a settled plan, they steadily persisted in their endeavours to undermine it, each of the party pegging away at him in his or her particular fashion.

Julius, who said little in public, would attack him privately, under the friendly veil of tobacco.

"You and I are too old to make new friends, old fellow," he would urge, "so we must even settle down within hail of one another. And your old craze, if a trifle subdued, is still in working order, as I know very well. You'll never be happy without a community of some sort to work for and worry over, and here's a place ready and willing to let you slave in its interests, now that it has learned to understand you. Why, man, you'd take at least a decade to work any new district up to this pitch of receptivity!"

"Why not settle on your mother's old family estate," the squire kept asking, "and oust that intriguing Lady Bountiful of ours, who does a deal more harm than people imagine? Her lease is up in six or eight months, I believe; now, why not offer to release her for the remainder of her term, and live at the Manor House yourself, among your own tenants and people? It's my opinion that Mrs. French-Chichester is staying up in town now merely to avoid you. And if you would but take root here, maybe we should be rid of that dangerous woman for good."

"Little Rose should be educated at home," that was Kate's string, and she harped on it constantly.

Now, which of these argumentative

weapons gave the final stroke of grace to his old resolution Simon was never brought to admit; but somehow or other his scheme of a second expatriation came to be quashed. If questioned about it, he would aver that his change of mind must have been due to the weather; for when he at length succumbed, the early summertide was just settling down sweetly and shyly upon lush pasture and flower-trimmed hedge and all the bosky curvings of the Chilling gorge; and he freely confessed that he had seen nothing abroad to compare with this "old June weather" in the old country.

Mrs. French-Chichester consented to forego the remainder of her lease for a consideration, and resumed her *rôle* of Lady Bountiful in another part of the country; whereupon Simon took possession of his mother's old home.

This definite home-coming of Sir Simon Secretan made a considerable stir in the neighbourhood, and he soon found the old life, or rather a revised and improved version of the same, sitting comfortably upon him, like some old garment, once cast aside as a miss-fit, but now donned afresh with satisfaction. Whether the old garment had been cut to his shape, or his own figure had undergone a change, he did not stop to consider, but wisely consented to live his life and enjoy it. He accepted the captaincy of the cricket club, which Lord Bridistow had long held in trust for him, and the presidency of the angling association, as also several other posts which were always open to any one willing to give time and money for the benefit of his neighbours.

Then there only remained for this reclaimed prodigal to take to himself a wife, and certainly a friendly neighbourhood seemed bent upon thus crowning his happiness.

For a time, it is true, people held aloof

under an impression that he would now revive his old inclination for the lady whom he had jilted, or who had jilted him—nobody quite knew which. But before long it became apparent that he had quite got over that ancient weakness. He met Nell in society several times, and the pair were at first scrutinized with deep interest; but there was nothing in their conduct calculated to cause the least uneasiness to any possessor of marriageable daughters.

Kate remarked, however, that as time went on Nell and Simon did attain to a certain mild degree of mutual friendliness. It being the summer season, when the countryside woke up according to custom, and betook itself to gentle outdoor dissipations, and Simon being at this time in great request, and really minded to see something of his neighbours, it naturally happened that the pair came across one another with some frequency. Yet no one could say that Simon exerted himself in the smallest degree to bring about these meetings. He was willing enough, in his present genial frame of mind, to support the boredom of a garden-party, but the presence or absence of Nell thereat seemed in no wise to affect his spirits.

" The fact is "—thus Kate summed up the situation one morning after discussing it at some length with her husband and the squire —" the fact is, Nell and Simon have now reached the highest pitch of intimacy that they will permit themselves ; and I've quite made up my mind that nothing will ever come of it."

" Have you ? " asked Julius ironically. " Permit me to doubt that ; for a woman's romantic hope has ninety times nine lives. In fact, nothing will ever kill it. You'd hope on, my dear, were these two tottering grey-headed to their respective graves. How often have I insisted that Simon isn't one to take up another man's leavings, the fractions of a woman's heart, and 'orts of her love'? And where's the necessity of marrying him at all? Let him live in peace and forget his old troubles, instead of planting a fresh crop."

"You're really mistaken," Kate insisted. " I have no more hope whatever of destroying Simon's peace in that way."

"But I have," put in the old squire; "and I'm not agoing to drop it to please that captious fellow Julius."

They both turned to laugh at the old gentleman; and Julius pressed with mock eagerness for an explanation.

"You shan't bully me into giving reasons for my view of the case," chuckled Mr. Rush; "but maybe I have one or two, though I don't pretend to be as clever as you young people. You let me alone, and happen I shall triumph over you both one of these fine days?"

"Look at the group of aspens yonder,"

quoth Kate, pointing through the breakfast-room window. "Do you perceive how fast they're mellowing? Well, when Simon first arrived they were hardly in full leaf; and do you suppose he would be all these months getting to the point of a mere cool friendship if he had any warmer feeling to bestow?"

"Don't you be too clever, and logical, and all that, Kate, for I'm not agoing to argue with you. You just give me that note for your sister, if it's done, and in an hour or so I'll take it over to the hall, for Mrs. Nell and I are great friends, and I'm always glad of an excuse for a chat with her."

Later on the squire took Kate's note, and drove away to Monks Damerel.

As he passed through the gates into the main road, and turned his head for a glance back at the house, the old man's face wore a tranquil and happy smile. There was a time, in the consulship of Children and McTavish, when he had hated his home, and dreaded returning to it after an hour's drive; now the Bickington roof covered almost everything his heart could desire.

There was the once terrible Kate, now converted into a kind and affectionate daughter; there was the beloved son, whose countenance he had once been glad to look upon for some four weeks out of the fifty-two, now safely captured and contently established for life beneath his own vine and fig-tree; and up at the nursery window his old eyes could just distinguish the figure of the curly headed little grandson for whom he had yearned so long and so ardently.

Around him the October sunshine was brooding over stubble and pasture, over quiet homesteads and rick-yards full of piled-up gold, and the solemn tenderness of the waning year wove itself into his thoughts as he drove gently along. To the westward of his route the smoke of Holla-comb Manor rose from its dense hanging woods; before him the great moorland spurs which shut in Monks Damerel loomed through the warm autumnal haze. He naturally fell to thinking of Simon and Nell, and wondering whether Hollacomb and Monks Damerel would really come together, according to his hopeful forecast.

The squire was tolerably certain that he had seen deeper into the returned exile's mind than either his son or daughter had done, and that Simon's former sentiments towards Nell had really undergone no change; but he was equally sure that the man's stubborn pride would have nothing to say to offers of friendship or gratitude. The question was whether Nell would have anything better to bestow upon her old lover; and the squire had lately been inclined to answer this in the affirmative. For, as a much keener observer than most people imagined, he had gathered an impression that Simon's coldness was in fact in the nature of a well-considered, masterly neglect, which was slowly but surely doing its work with the young widow.

Upon reaching the hall the visitor was informed that Mrs. Clancy was in the old garden, somewhere in the direction of the bowling-green, whither he at once proceeded in search of her.

Through the pleached alleys of the formal garden the old man paced reflectively along, enjoying its sheltered quietude, and holding Kate's note in his hand for fear of forgetting it.

He presently emerged through an opening in the great yew hedge on to the little raised terrace which ran round the bowling-green; and thereupon a curious feeling that he had walked clean out of real life into a fairy-tale took possession of him.

The green was partly shaded by some ancient ash trees, but was open on the south side, where a low wall bordered the

terrace without interrupting the view of combe and moorland which it commanded. Seated close to the wall, with the mild sunshine flowing round her, was the young widow, with a table and some books at her elbow. Before her, a six-year-old figure, quaintly attired in dead gold and amber as though to match the rich colour-chords of the fading season, was playing on the green with a ball and some big nine-pins. On the edge of the grass stood a tall man, watching the busy little figure and placidly smoking.

The visitor paused for a moment as though loth to disturb this idyllic group.

What struck him especially was that they all seemed engaged in ordinary occupations. It seemed improbable that Simon could have come over just once in a way, or that Rose was engaged in a new game, or that Nell was in the position of a hostess receiving unusual visitors. Judging from the everyday atmosphere of the scene the squire was inclined to infer that it had been enacted a good many times before; and he soon found his guess to be a correct one.

Nell greeted him cordially as usual, drawing a chair for the old squire beside her own; and he settled down with a feeling that he was joining a family party.

Little Rose's prattle quickly disclosed the fact that this game on the bowling-green was, in fine weather, the ordinary sequel to her morning's lessons; that, her books once laid aside, she and Simon were in the habit of crossing the brook, which separated the two properties on this side, and making their way hither by a steep path through the woods.

Thus it was clear that Simon and Nell were a good deal more intimate than their observant neighbours and critics were at all aware of. On the other hand, it was equally evident to the squire that they were not lovers. The unexpected visitor's presence gave them no embarrassment whatever ; nothing approaching to a tender glance passed between them ; nor did Simon's manner exhibit any symptom of a lover's elation. In fact, it soon appeared that his mood was of rather a gloomy shade this morning.

From the conversation that followed the new arrival gathered that Mrs. Clancy and little Rose had been developing a mutual friendship lately, and could now hardly see enough of each other. It seemed that Simon, as has been said, brought the child over almost every morning for half an hour or so, and that she came again with her governess for a longer visit later in the day. The inquisitive old gentleman elicited these details by innocent little questions ; he also ascertained that the little programme had been followed for some weeks.

This explanation, he considered, betrayed rather a droll and piquant state of things, of

which even Kate had not the least conception. It delighted him to think how Simon
had been over-reaching all his sharp-eyed
neighbours ; yet—yet the man puzzled him
somehow. Simon's manner was almost harsh
to Nell; he seemed to take a pleasure in
differing from everything she said, and in
drawing little Rose away every time she
made a remark to her. Nell seemed pained
and depressed at his unfriendliness ; and the
squire fancied he could detect in her something approaching to jealousy of Simon's
affection for the child. She had the air of
one who was being purposely kept out in
the cold.

"Strange, strange," muttered the looker-
on. "I don't seem to understand the man
a bit, for all my boasting ; and Nell is in
the same predicament. She looked pensive
and depressed, poor child, from the first;
and now he's making her worse every
minute."

"Ah, you want to go home, do you, Miss Fickle?" said Simon presently, swinging the child to the ground. "There, run and tell Mrs. Clancy you're tired of her already. Take the opportunity of being candid while you're young, for they'll never let you speak the truth when you're a grown woman."

"I'm tired of you already," said the child obediently, holding out a morsel of a hand to Nell.

Simon laughed harshly. The gentle old squire was deeply shocked, especially when he saw Nell's dark eyes filling.

"Oh, poor Mrs. Clancy—you mustn't be so unkind to her, Rose!" he cried hastily.

But Simon only laughed again.

"We're all alike, you see," he remarked carelessly; "nothing pleases any one of us but change. That is the only secret of happiness. Rasselas might have discovered so much without fagging about among all sorts and conditions of people as he did. Look at me

now. I'm hardly yet settled in at Hollacomb, yet already growing restless. This
sober, pensive kind of weather bores me.
There's no variety, no excitement in this
dead-alive old country. Is a man to spend
his life shooting corn-fed pheasants, and
dining with neighbours who are already
growing sick of him, boring others as
thoroughly as he bores himself? In a year's
time, Miss Fickle, yea, in half a year's time,
I expect we shall begin our wanderings
again. We'll look in at the Cape for a month
or two; then, when the inevitable weariness
and staleness supervene, move on to New
Zealand, as we did before—and so on, and
so on; following the old round, accepting the
fact that life's a poor dish at best, and change
the only salt that makes its flavour tolerable."

"I'm not tired yet—I'll give you a kiss,
Mrs. C'ancy," murmured Rose, approaching
Nell as though she thought her in need of
sympathy.

"You little humbug, don't pretend to be sentimental, when the only thing you really care for is your grub !"

"Don't put her against me," entreated Nell, "for I assure you that I have few enough friends."

"Oh, everybody labours under that sentimental impression," Simon retorted impatiently, "the truth being that there's no such thing as friendship. We find a man a good listener, or a possessor of the same prejudices as ourselves, or in some way or other gifted with a power of ministering to our vanity and egoism, and we call him 'friend;' and he gives us the same meaningless title on like selfish grounds. And when either party dies, the other says, 'Poor devil!'—and goes on with his book or newspaper."

Nell was now bending over the child, placing the small arms round her own neck. The squire was hovering over her, at intervals throwing a fierce glance at her tormentor; while Simon strode up and down, with the aspect of one who is giving his mind to making other people as miserable as himself.

"Why—you're crying, aren't you?" whispered little Rose in a wondering tone.

Certainly Mrs. Clancy's cheek had a tear on it, and the tender-hearted old man was up in arms immediately.

"You shouldn't pour out your evil thoughts in that harsh, reckless way, Simon," he cried wrathfully. "You've no right to hurt people's feelings in this wanton manner. You make me quite wretched, you do, with your cynical remarks. And you can't mean 'em—you can't dare to mean 'em! Look at your friendship for my son—is that all a sham and a delusion?"

"I don't suppose my friendship for Julius will suffice to keep me another day in this country, once I've got thoroughly bored, squire." Simon was now leaning moodily

difficulty—"as you've been a-treating our kind, and dear, and gentle Nell—for—for ever so!"

Nell smiled upon her protector, but his sympathy tended to further upset her self-control. She turned away, and leaned over the low wall as Simon had done a short time since.

"But you don't really care whether I go or not?" asked Simon.

She made no answer. They saw that she was crying.

Then the old man's wrath melted suddenly away, for he perceived a sudden change in Simon's face. There was a gleam of strange happiness in the big man's eyes. He looked as though he were about to step forward and catch the slight figure from the low wall to his heart and never let it go again.

Noting which, the squire walked away along the terrace on tiptoe, feeling somewhat unhinged, yet with a glow of deep satisfaction spreading through him. He knew that his triumph over Kate and Julius was now an assured thing. It might not come yet, there might be months to wait; but he no longer felt any doubt as to its final consummation.

"I'll keep it dark," he muttered, "I'll not tell even Kate. She deserves to be kept out in the cold for her scepticism. How long will it be, I wonder? Will they come to an understanding before the leaves are quite gone?"

He turned for a final glance before passing through the opening in the yew hedge.

Simon had drawn no nearer to Nell. He was standing a little apart, waiting for her to recover, holding his little charge by the hand. The mild sunlight was bathing the old green, and the terrace, and the three figures by the wall.

"Well, I'll give them till Christmas," concluded the departing squire.

But this old man with the young heart

was a little premature in his forecast; for
the ash trees overhanging the bowling-green
were budding once more, and the birds in
the combe below were singing spring pæans
on the morning of his final triumph over his
son and daughter.

THE END.

PRINTED BY WILLIAM CLOWES AND SONS, LIMITED,
LONDON AND BECCLES.   *S. & H.*